Joseph Fitzgerald Molloy

The Life and Adventures of Peg Woffington

With pictures of the period in which she lived. Vol. 1

Joseph Fitzgerald Molloy

The Life and Adventures of Peg Woffington
With pictures of the period in which she lived. Vol. 1

ISBN/EAN: 9783744790604

Printed in Europe, USA, Canada, Australia, Japan

Cover: Foto ©Raphael Reischuk / pixelio.de

More available books at **www.hansebooks.com**

M.ʳˢ WOFFINGTON.

THE

LIFE AND ADVENTURES

OF

PEG WOFFINGTON

WITH PICTURES OF THE PERIOD
IN WHICH SHE LIVED

BY

J. FITZGERALD MOLLOY

In Two Volumes

VOL. I.

NEW YORK
DODD, MEAD, AND COMPANY
1892

University Press:

JOHN WILSON AND SON, CAMBRIDGE, U. S. A.

TO MISS ELLEN TERRY.

DEAR MADAM, — The brilliant actress who forms the subject of these pages rendered such service to the drama in the past century as entitles her to a prominent position in its annals. You as a distinguished artist have achieved such histrionic triumphs in the present century as shall render your name illustrious in the same history.

Seldom, if indeed ever, has such a happy trinity of genius, grace, and beauty been united in one person. The perfection and tenderness of your tragedy, the justness and brilliancy of your comedy are alike subjects on which innumerable pens have discoursed with vast pleasure; themes on which all who have witnessed your performances have dwelt with uncommon satisfaction. You have idealized your personations; you have realized the highest poetical conceptions; you have delighted the most cultured intelligences of two worlds.

As a testimony though most poor, as a tribute though most slight, to the incalculable services you have rendered unto art, I gladly avail myself of your permission to dedicate to you the labor of many months, to inscribe your illustrious name on the titlepage of these volumes.

Faithfully yours always,

J. FITZGERALD MOLLOY.

PREFACE.

NO biography of Peg Woffington, the most brilliant actress of her century, has up to this time been written. Her very name might have been forgotten had not a great novelist rescued her memory from oblivion and directed interest to her career. Yet this has been achieved by the aid of fiction, as he acknowledged to me a little while before laying down his pen for ever. But Charles Reade, as was to be expected from a master-hand, struck the proper keynote of her life in the novel which bears the great actress's name ; so that though the scenes by which he surrounded her are imaginary, they are yet in perfect harmony with her character.

Indeed, there was scarce necessity to borrow colours from fiction wherewith to brighten the portrait of one whose life was in itself a romance.

I have endeavoured in the following pages to give this portrait as caught in transitory glances afforded by the oftentimes curt and scattered mention of her name in the biographies, letters, journals, and criticisms of her contemporaries ; just as by the occasional opening of a door one without an apartment obtains glimpses of a striking figure passing in the crowd within. But these have been sufficient, if not to present an etching, at least to give a portrait, faithful in its lines, though not lacking hues beseeming subjects purely ideal.

As an actress she was the most central figure in her brief bright day, and as such I have presented her, surrounded by a brilliant group of players, wits, critics, men of fashion and of letters, who were her friends or her contemporaries. The remaining space on the canvas I have filled in with views of town life as it was in her day ; for encircled by such personages, and seen against the lights and shadows of such a background, she can alone be properly estimated.

Concerning David Garrick, who for a time played an important part in the drama of her life, and who occupied so prominent a position in the history of the stage in the middle of the last century, I have found much to say. Moreover, I have been enabled to give some letters concerning his early life, and the feelings with which his adoption of the stage were received by his family. Portions of some of these have been given in the later editions of Mr. Forster's ' Life of Oliver Goldsmith ; ' but they have never before been printed in full, and will, I trust, prove entertaining to that very considerable section of the public concerned in aught regarding the history of the theatre.

The task of giving sketches of the numerous characters introduced in these pages, sufficiently vivid to interest, yet necessarily brief with regard to the limits of the volumes, is one which will be readily recognised as fraught with difficulty ; but labour has not been spared in striving to render the book acceptable to a public which has already extended a kindly appreciation to similar efforts.

J. FITZGERALD MOLLOY.

List of Illustrations.

CONTENTS TO VOL. I.

CHAPTER I.

CHAPTER II.

CHAPTER III.

CHAPTER IV.

CHAPTER V.

CHAPTER VI.

CHAPTER VII.

CHAPTER VIII.

CHAPTER IX.

The Life and Adventures

OF

PEG WOFFINGTON.

CHAPTER I.

The little Water-carrier and the Foreign Lady. — Madame Vio-
lante and Mrs. Woffington. — Pupil to a Dancer. — The
Booth in Fownes Court. — Little Peg in 'The Beggars'
Opera.' — Charles Kelly and 'The Devil to Pay.' — At the
Aungier Street Playhouse. — Dancing between the Acts. —
Playing Ophelia, her Beauty and her Triumph. — The Part
of Phillis. — Falling in Love. — A Young Gentleman of
Quality and his Ways. — A Journey to London Town.

A T the close of an October day in the year
1727, a child of about eight years old
slowly tottered along Ormond Quay, Dublin,
under the weight of a pitcher of water which
she carried on her head. The evening had set
in dark and cold, and promised a bleak and
dreary night. Already the sky was overcast
with heavy clouds ; a sad-voiced northeast
wind, sweeping up the sluggish Liffey, carried
with it a chill, penetrating mist, that gradually
increased to drenching rain. Heavily framed

I. — I

lamps, imprisoning the poor, wan light of oil
wicks, swung with many a creak from the corner houses of dreary streets and black-looking
alleys, or hung above the old stone bridges
with quaint and ponderous balustrades, and
buttresses green and slimy from the ebb and
flow of countless tides, casting a patch of light
upon the black waters beneath, as if seeking
crimes and mysteries hidden in their depths.
A few passengers, with heads bowed low and
cloaks and coats drawn tightly round them to
avoid the bitter wind, hastened to and fro,
shadow-like, in the deepening gloom. A coach
or two rattled with noisy haste over the uneven
pavements. The bells of the church clocks rang
out six, their sounds falling faint and changeful,
like frightened voices crying for help from the
heights of steeples and towers upon which the
vapour and cloud had already descended.

With the wind blowing in her face, the rain
dashing on her scarcely covered limbs, the child,
labouring under the weight of her pitcher, made
but slow way. At last, shivering in her wet
rags, and overcome by her misery, she burst
into tears, raised her arms above her head,
removed the pitcher, and sought the passing
shelter of an open doorway. She had scarcely
wiped the rain from her face with the remains

of an old tattered and colourless shawl which helped to cover her shoulders, when a lady, who had for some time followed her, also sought protection in the hall, faintly lit by the flickering rays of a lamp.

'You are cold, my childe,' said the lady, looking at her keenly.

'Yes, ma'am,' said the girl, raising her eyes, expressive of surprise, to the stranger's face.

Even in her rags the child looked picturesque. Her dark unkempt hair curled naturally round a well-shaped head, and hung above a wide, low forehead ; her eyes, large and liquid, seemed almost black under the shadow of their long lashes and the full, sweeping curve of her brows ; her cheeks were pale and beautifully oval, her lips somewhat full and red ; whilst her prettily dimpled chin gave a piquant look to the lower part of her face, which the sweet gravity of her eyes contradicted.

'And what is your name, my leetle childe ?' said the lady, in a voice to which a foreign accent gave a peculiar softness.

'Me name is Peg, ma'am,' said the girl, opening wide her eyes, made all the brighter by the tears which yet glistened in them.

'Peg ; it is a pretty name. But is there no other ?' asked the lady, pushing back the dark, tangled locks with a touch that was caressing in its gentleness.

'Peg Woffington, ma'am,' said the girl, pleased with the lady's attentions.

'And where you live, eh, leetle Peg Woffing-ton? Is it far from here, eh?' continued the foreign lady, letting her eyes wander from the child's handsome face to her limbs, rounded and shaped with wonderful grace.

'Not far, ma'am,' said Peg. 'Me mother lives in George's Court. She is a widee, an' she washes for the neighbours;' and so saying, she cast her eyes on the pitcher of water by her side, as if some train of thought had suddenly suggested itself to her mind. 'An' this is washing-day, an' I've been carryin' jugs o' water since dinner. But this is the last of 'em an' — an' I must go now, ma'am; for there's no sign o' the rain stoppin', an' mother will be wonderin' what keeps me,' said Peg, stooping to raise her burden on her head once more.

'And I shall go with you,' said the lady, with that foreign accent which gave her voice so sweet a sound.

The child set the pitcher down again, straightened herself, and looked at the lady with eyes expressive of wonder.

' I am,' said the lady, ' Madame Violante.
You perhaps have heard my name ? '

' What ! ' said Peg, in greater amazement
now than ever ; for at the mention of that
name there rose before her a vision of a great
booth in Fownes Court, with a vast glare of
lights, where the sounds of fiddles and drums
were heard strumming and beating right merry
measures, and to which crowds flocked nightly,
that they might see such tricks and daring feats
as had never before been witnessed in this
goodly city.

' And you are Madame 'Lante, that dances
on the rope ? ' said Peg, looking down at the
lady's feet, as if by her glance she would un-
ravel the great mystery by which the celebrated
dancer nightly balanced herself on a tight-rope
and skipped upon a slack-wire above the heads
of applauding crowds.

' The same,' said the French lady, smiling.
' Would you like to dance also on the rope — '

' And wear such beautiful dresses, with span-
gles ? ' interrupted this juvenile daughter of Eve.
' Oh, ma'am, I would be delighted ! '

' Very well, I will teach you,' said Violante.

' And shall I wear a star on me forehead,
ma'am, when I dance, like you ? ' she asked.

' Yes,' answered Madame Violante, ' if you

learn quickly and well. But first we must ask
your mother, and hear what she will say ; show
me the way to her house, and whilst we go you
can tell me all about yourself, my childe.'

So Peg lifted the earthenware pitcher, that
seemed now no heavier than a feather, and
placed it on her shapely head, and went out
into the darkness which was almost as of night.
Her steps were so light and quick that her new
friend could scarcely keep pace with her ; the
rain and wind were unheeded, though the one
pattered on her face and the other sent the
poor rags fluttering from her rounded limbs.
Presently they left the exposed quays and
turned up a dark, narrow street, with high,
black-looking houses on either side, in the
friendly shelter of which the child, in answer to
the Frenchwoman's questions, told her that she
and her mother and her little sister were as
poor as church mice, since, said she, ' the doctors, the devil take 'em, killed me father when
he had the faver a few years ago ; an' sure,
't was the first time in his life he ever had 'em
to attend him, and 't was his last. God be
good to his sowl ! but they say the doctors
are never lucky, and they kill a mighty lot o'
people, anyhow. An' me mother,' she continued, ' takes in washin', an' works hard all

day ; an' at night she sells oranges outside the
doors o' the playhouse in Aungier Street, an'
never a much she makes be that same ; an'
as for meself, sometimes I sell oranges too,
an' sallad for a ha'penny a dish, an' water-
cresses in the sayson ; and the young gentlemen in Trinity College behave dacent to me,
an' often give me a penny for nothin' at all,
only because I talk to them an' make them
laugh ; an' they 're not bad, poor fellows, anyhow, when they have the money ; but sure,
there are times when they 're just as poor as
meself, a'most, an' it 's many a time I popped
their clothes for them, comin' to the end o'
the month, you know. But they 're rale good-
hearted, an' they like me well.'

At the end of this dark street they turned
into a lane on the right, and finally entered an
unsavoury court, lighted only by the dim rays
of tallow candles shining through the small-
paned windows of the surrounding hovels.
Quickly gliding into one of them, the child
mounted a rickety stair, loudly calling out to
her mother that a lady was coming to see her.
At this information, a woman wearing a deep-
bordered blowsy cap that had once been white,
and a cotton gown, the sleeves of which were
rolled to the shoulders, displaying her red and

smoky arms fresh from the wash-tub, hastily took
a candle from a tin sconce nailed to the white-
washed wall. and rushing forward with it, held
it above the creaking stairway, in a position
most favourable to the descent of melted tallow
on her visitor's head.

'Walk in, ma'am, an' welcome,' said the
hostess, foreseeing in her mind's eye an additional customer to the wash-tub. Restoring
the candle to the sconce, she made a rush at
the best chair the poor room contained, and
rubbed it heartily with her apron, which she
afterwards applied in the same manner to her
perspiring face.

'An' won't you sit down, ma'am?' she continued, peering into the stranger's countenance
through an atmosphere which was rendered a
trifle misty by smoke from the turf fire and
steam from the wash-tub. 'Peg, stir the cra-
dle, and don't let Polly wake. Do you hear
me?'

'Mother,' said Peg, feeling herself called
on to make some introduction, 'it's Madame
'Lante,' adding, after a moment's pause, 'the
lady that dances on the rope.' And so saying,
the child made a curtsey, not without grace, to
her visitor.

Being favoured with this introduction, the

danseuse seated herself and explained the motive of her visit. She had been struck by the
beauty of Peg's face, and by the grace and
bearing of her figure, and offered to take her
as an apprentice and teach her the business of
a tight-rope dancer. The poor washerwoman
dried her arms, opened her eyes very wide, and
looked bewildered at the unexpected proposal
which was so suddenly laid before her.

' It will be well for the leetle Peg ; she will
earn good salaries in a short times,' put in
Madame Violante, ' and I will dress and support her.'

At this prospect a shrewd twinkle came into
Mrs. Woffington's eyes. She knew the value
of money.

' Well, ma'am,' she said, putting her arms
akimbo, ' none of me blood has ever been play-
actors, or ever danced upon a rope ; an' for the
matter o' that, me mother's people never dis-
graced themselves be earning a penny piece,
but lived upon their own 'states like the highest in the land ; an' sure, 't was often tould
us the head of the family was one o' the rale
kings of Ireland himself. But sure, that was
in the good owld times, and there 's no use
in talking o' them ; and here am I, only a poor
widee-woman, God help me ! with two children

to support, an' the times mighty hard, an' me
good man took from me with little or no warn-
ing, God help us ! An' its a miserable world
we live in.'

' It was sad,' the sympathetic Frenchwoman
said, taking advantage of a slight pause in the
widow's autobiographical sketch.

' An' sure, every one knows, ma'am,' she
continued, ' that you bear the character of an
honest woman, an' not like most o' them
wenches belonging to the playhouse. An'
sure, as you say Peggy might earn a dacent
livin' in a little while, an' that you will support
and clothe the child, sure you may take her,
an' I 'll pray God to protect her,' said the
washerwoman.

So it was settled that Peg was to become
one of Madame's pupils ; and in a little while,
attired in long drawers, short jacket, and flat
pumps, she learned to dance and skip about the
stage, and presently to sing songs ; for all of
which she was duly admired by the frequenters
of the booth, who flung her showers of pence,
which she quickly picked up and duly gave
to her mother. But public taste is proverbially
fickle. Although such surprising performances
on the tight-rope as Madame Violante's had
never been seen in Dublin before, yet there

JOHN GAY ESQ.ᵣ

was a monotony about them which palled after
a while, and by degrees the pleasant booth in
Fownes Court, with its sconces of tallow lights,
its fiddles, its drums, its merry dances, and its
aërial performances, became deserted. Now
Madame Violante was a woman of enterprise
and energy, and no sooner did one attraction
fail to fill her coffers than she quickly looked
about her for another ; and, like those who
seek in earnest, she found it in good time.

But a little before, all theatrical London had
been in a state of intense excitement concerning a performance called ' The Beggars' Opera,'
by the poet Gay. It had been produced by
Rich, then manager of Lincoln's Inn Fields
Theatre, and had been played for sixty-two
consecutive nights, ' making Rich gay, and Gay
rich.' The opera was furthermore notable as
being the occasion of a drawn battle between
George II. and her Grace the mad Duchess
of Queensbury ; which of course added to its
notoriety considerably. Now this comic opera
had never been heard or witnessed in Dublin,
though the report of its sparkling dialogue, its
genuine wit and satirical ditties, had of course
crossed the Channel. It therefore struck Madame Violante to form a company of children,
instruct them in the parts of this opera, and have

it performed in her booth. The idea was no
sooner conceived than acted upon, and in a
little while the Dublin public was invited to
witness the results of her training.

The principal character, Polly, was given to
Peg Woffington ; and strange to say, not only
she, but almost all the children who personated
the characters in this opera, afterwards became
celebrated actors and actresses. Madame Violante, meanwhile, moved to a more commodious
booth in George's Court, which on the night of
the first performance of ' The Beggars' Opera '
was prodigiously crowded. Amongst the audience sat a goodly number of Peg's old friends
and admirers from Trinity College, who, when
this lovely girl with the blue-black hair and
liquid eyes came forward looking pale from
fright, received her with an ovation that set her
nervousness to flight and gave her hope of much
forbearance. The charm of her face. the beauty
of her limbs, the natural grace of her movements, would, if such were necessary, have
compensated for much that was crude to a
people ever keenly sensitive to the effects of
physical gifts. But her crudities were scarcely
perceptible ; and when the curtain fell that
night, the young actress had the satisfaction of
knowing that her first appearance in what may

be called an important part gave promise of future success. In those old days and good there existed a common feeling of friendship between performers and their audiences, which was productive of many advantages to both ; and in accordance with the custom of the times, at the conclusion of the opera Madame Violante stepped forward from the world behind the scenes to receive the congratulations of her patrons on her financial success, as well as on the result of the training of her troupe.

Little Peg Woffington also descended into the commonplace world, by means of a half-dozen creaking steps, to receive her meed of praise before joining her mother, who, hoarse from crying oranges at the door of the booth, was now awaiting her daughter, with her empty basket on her arm, a comfortable sense of proprietorship in her manner, and a glow of pride in her honest face, — round, rubicund, and set in a framework of blowsy borders.　Now, amongst those who most warmly congratulated Peg and her patroness was Mr. Charles Coffey, — a little, wiry, dark-complexioned man, who looked as if he were being half-strangled by his high collar and many-folded cravat.　His meagre frame was clad in a black body-coat ; his lower limbs in velvet breeches fastened at the knee by rows of brass buttons and bows of black ribbon, and in worsted stockings that betrayed a lamentable lack of calf. For all that, it was easily seen that Mr. Charles Coffey was a man of parts, and likewise of vast importance ; for he was the composer of ‘ The Beggars’ Wedding,’ a ballad opera of great humour, which had met with prodigious success, if not in Dublin, at least in London, where it had been performed for thirty consecutive nights at the Haymarket, and had likewise held the boards of Covent Garden and the great Drury Lane playhouse itself. Moreover, he had likewise written, or rather plagiarised, a ballad farce rejoicing in the comprehensive title, ‘ The Devil to Pay,’ which had also met with great applause at Drury Lane, and to which Miss Raftor (known afterwards as Kitty Clive) owed vast obligations, as it afforded her scope for the display of the comic talents which the world was not aware she possessed till then.

Now it pleased Mr. Charles Coffey to graciously offer to instruct Peg Woffington in the part of Nell in his new ballad farce, — the character in which Kitty Raftor had won her laurels. He had closely studied the Drury Lane actress, until her every whimsical movement and humourous expression were stamped

on his mind ; and these he was ready to teach
Peggy, in order that his farce might meet a
success in his native town, in which he was no
prophet, such as it had already received in the
greater capital.

At this proposal both Peg and her mistress
were delighted ; she was apt, studied hard, and
made a sensation in the part when the ballad
farce was duly produced in Madame Violante's
canvas-covered booth. From this hour she was
looked on as a prodigy, destined for renown
some day, and was sought after by the polite
circles of the town. From association with
such society, she, being imitative and impres-
sionable, quickly learned to act in accordance
with its genteel manners, just as she had rapidly learned singing from Charles Coffey and
French from Madame Violante.

For a considerable time the charming Peggy
acted small parts, sang ballads, and danced
jigs under Madame Violante's management ;
but fate proving unkind to this lady, her business declined, and she was obliged to let her
booth. But Peg's reputation as a clever and
accomplished young actress had meanwhile
risen, and her services were sought for by
Elrington, then manager of the Theatre Royal,
as the Aungier Street playhouse was called,

where she sang in operas and farces, and
danced with great grace between the acts, in
company with Monsieur Moreau and Mr.
William Delemain. It was not, however, until February, 1737, that she was permitted to
make her appearance in what is known as 'a
speaking character.' The accident which gave
her this chance was the same which has afforded
similar opportunities to many actresses who have
afterwards become known to fame. The play
of 'Hamlet,' 'written by the famous Shakespeare,' was announced for performance at the
Theatre Royal. Two days before that on which
the tragedy was to be produced, the lady selected to play the part of Ophelia fell ill ; when
Peg came forward and offered to undertake
the character. Elrington in return laughed at
her proposal ; but nothing daunted, she offered
to repeat some of Ophelia's lines for his benefit, the result being that Miss Woffington was
announced in the bills to play the part of this
woe-stricken heroine.

She had long ago become a favourite with the
public, and the event of her making her appearance in this important character caused a vast
excitement to her patrons in particular, and the
town in general. True to their natural characteristic love of display, the good citizens of

Dublin were excessively fond of playhouses. On friendly personal terms with most of the actors and actresses, they were familiar with every event of their lives, and dealt out to them from pit and gallery their favour or displeasure, if with occasional indiscretion, at least with an openness that left no doubt as to their prejudices. Peg Woffington had been known to them from the days when she had sold salad and water-cresses in the streets, and the town regarded her with especial favour; her appearance in so prominent a part as that of Ophelia was therefore looked forward to with unusual interest, and on the evening of the 17th of February the Aungier Street playhouse was crowded from pit to gallery to witness her performance. Seldom had there been seen so brilliant a house, or one more keenly, nay, anxiously, attentive; and when at length Ophelia came forward, her dark eyes luminous with excitement, her beautiful face pale from fear, she held her audience as by a spell, which the justness of her expression and grace of her manner heightened as the play proceeded. When the curtain descended on the mad-scene, it was felt that she had secured a triumph which was not only complete in itself, but gave promise of great achievements in the future.

I. — 2

From this date she no longer danced between the acts or sang ballads in small parts.
It was her ambition to climb the ladder of theatrical fame ; and once having gained a step,
she was not the woman to descend to her former level.   Her next important part was that
of Phillis in Sir Richard Steele's ' Conscious
Lovers,' and was almost as great a success as
her representation of Ophelia.   For two sea-
sons she played leading parts, bringing large
audiences and full coffers to the Aungier Street
playhouse, — gaining especial renown in the
part of Sir Harry Wildair, an elegant young
man of fashion.   This character she had attempted at the desire of several persons of consequence ; and so piquant and full of witchery
was her personation of the fashionable rake,
that she charmed the town to an uncommon
degree.

About this time an event happened which
may be considered the turning-point in her career : she fell in love.   The object of her affection was a young gentleman of position but
of small fortune, named Taaffe, — the third son
of a needy Irish peer.   He was not only delighted with her talents as an actress, but fascinated by her beauty as a woman.   He was
a man well to look upon, — tall and of goodly

shape, with sea-blue eyes, light-brown hair, and
a smile as bright, if, alas! as deceptive, as April
sunshine. Night after night he sat in the boxes
of the theatre, watching the play of her face that
was more beautiful than health, the glamour of
her lustrous eyes, the smiles that played round
a mouth like unto a cleft pomegranate, the turn
of her head, the movement of her graceful limbs.
When she left the stage, he felt as if sudden
darkness had descended upon him. She was to
him what sunlight is to the world. By day he
wooed her with soft words and gentle looks
and many endearments, with all the passion,
the longing, and the pain of his youth ; for he
thought to himself no woman ever was born so
beautiful as she. And as a woman she loved him,
not wisely but too well, — trusting him with the
precious treasure of her honour, resting con-
fident that because of her vast affection for him
he would in return make her his lawful wife.
At his request she quitted the stage at a time
when the promise of a great career shone before
her ; at his desire she left her native city to
accompany him to London. For she loved him
all in all.

CHAPTER II.

In Merry London Town. — The King's Court and the Prince's.
— Views of the Streets. — The Coffee-houses and their Frequenters. — Round Covent Garden. — The Players' Quarters
and Clare Market. — Laws concerning the Playhouses and
their Audiences. — Dress of the Period. — Johnson, Garrick,
and Savage. — At the Fountain Tavern. — Visiting on ' Clean
Shirt Day.'— Reynolds, Pope, and Smollett. — Quin at Drury
Lane, Cibber at Covent Garden. — Vauxhall, its Ways and
its Visitors. — With Lady Caroline Petersham. — A Strange
Advertisement.

WHEN Peg Woffington arrived in town,
London was then, as it had been for the
last quarter of a century, the very centre of
gaiety and dissipation. The nobility were divided in their allegiance between the Court of
St. James, where George II., assisted by his
German mistress Madame Walmoden, created
Countess of Yarmouth, held drawing-rooms
twice a week, and Norfolk House, where
Frederick, Prince of Wales, an outcast from
the royal palace, had set up a court of his own,
where he and his brilliant followers gambled
and fiddled and danced and acted almost every
night throughout the year. The middle and
lower classes made merry over rumours that

reached them of the royal wrangles, but little heeding them, enjoyed themselves after their own fashion. The streets, with their steep-roofed, strangely carved, curiously gabled houses, crushing up against or overlapping each other in front by a foot or two, or lying snugly against deep-windowed, square-towered churches, were bright and busy all day long, — filled by a goodly crowd of courtiers and citizens, clad in many-coloured suits, all of whom were more or less known to each other, and exchanged salutations or civilities with a grace of movement and courtesy of speech lost to us in this latter day.

In the centre of the thoroughfares heavily built coaches, showily painted, emblazoned with coats-of-arms or coronets, lumbered along, — their slow way beset by carts or by hired chairs swinging between abusive-tongued chairmen, or by the chairs of persons of quality carried by livery-clad servants. To add, moreover, to the general obstruction of the narrow streets, barrows of fruits, vegetables, and edibles lined either side, as if to mark where the pavements should have been. Over the pedestrian's head, from above the doorway of almost every shop, hung strangely painted sign-boards, adorned with heraldic bearings, paintings of grotesque and fabulous animals, boars of many colours, or cocks

in legion, all of which swung and creaked threat-
eningly with every wind that swept from the
four corners of the globe.

All day long and far into the night the coffee-
houses, which were to be found in all quarters
of the town, were crowded by men of every
degree.   Those whose tastes or vocations took
them to St. James's or St. Paul's, alike used
them as places for the interchange of polite
conversation or the transaction of business.   In
these houses — the forerunners of clubs — the
frequenters paid a penny or twopence. according to the situation and circumstance of the
house, for a cup of good coffee ; which sum
likewise entitled the customer to read the broad-
sheets of the day, to linger for an hour or so
and hear the latest news from the court or the
city, the newest gossip from abroad, or from
the green-room of the Drury Lane playhouse,
or to enter into a discussion on the political
questions of the hour, the knavery of ministers
and the sycophancy of their followers.

There was Squire's Coffee House, a deep-
coloured red brick picturesque building, adjoining Gray's Inn Gate, which Sir Roger de
Coverley himself used to frequent in the first
decade of the century, when, seated at the
upper end of the room, at a high table, he

BUTTON.

would call for a clean pipe, a paper of tobacco,
a dish of coffee, a wax candle, and a newspaper,
with such an air of good-humour that everybody delighted in serving him. There was
Button's famous coffee-house in Russell Street,
Covent Garden, which Addison and his friends
had frequented, where Sir Richard Steele told
his wittiest story, where Dr. Garth uttered his
best pun, and which had been made the receiv-
ing-house for contributions to the ' Guardian,'
for which purpose a lion's head, designed by
Hogarth, had been put up as a letter-box ;
and likewise St. James's Coffee House, in
St. James's Street, where the Whigs gathered
and talked politics, and arranged the affairs of
Europe with a satisfaction heightened by sun-
dry pinches of Brazil snuff ; the same house
where Dean Swift—now dying in Ireland 'like
a rat in a hole,' as he expressed it — had
received his letters from poor broken-hearted
Stella, under cover to Joseph Addison, Esquire.
At the Grecian Coffee House handsome Jemmy
Maclaine, the celebrated highwayman, the son
of an Irish dean, the brother of a Calvinist
minister, might be seen any day, sipping his
coffee, making love to his landlord's daughter,
keeping an eye to his neighbour's property, and
joining in the conversation with vast polite-

ness, until one morning in May, 1750, when he
was hung on the charge of stealing a laced
waistcoat. In the open balcony at Toms' a
great crowd of noblemen adorned with their
stars and garters, and men of quality, might be
seen nightly, drinking their tea and coffee, exposed to the crowd. But the Bedford Coffee House, in Covent Garden, was more than
all others at this period signalized as the emporium of wit, the seat of criticism, and the
standard of taste. Here courtiers and citizens
met on common ground ; here, on the one
hand, the price of stocks was gravely discussed,
and on the other, Lord Chesterfield's last *bon
mot* was laughingly repeated. No student from
the universities launching himself on the world,
no lawyer's clerk clapping on a sword, no haber-
dasher's 'prentice donning a cue wig, but duly
put in an appearance at the Bedford, by way
of qualifying himself as a man about town. In
the little boxes, ranged round like hives, men
of every calling sipped their coffee nightly, dis-
cussing the affairs of the day, exchanging witti-
cisms, and narrating stories more laughable than
edifying. And wittiest among them all, creating
roars of laughter by his sallies or his mimicry
of some well-known actor or politician, was a
young gentleman of family and fortune, at this

MRS. PRITCHARD.

time a student of the Inner Temple. Dressed
in a frock-suit of green, and silver lace, bag
wig, sword, bouquet, and point ruffles, he frequented the place daily, until the carriage of
some woman of quality would drive to the
door, and Mr. Samuel Foote being inquired
for, he would hasten out, hat in hand, and ride
away with his lady fair.

Covent Garden in those days was a busy
hive, where not only coffee-houses, but gay
taverns and ordinaries and houses of dissipation
thickly clustered. At the ordinaries, dinners
were served at the rate of sixpence or a shilling
per head ; for the latter sum two courses being
supplied, — a goodly company, though somewhat mixed, gathering round the board. In
each of these houses a second apartment was
also set aside for the accommodation of the
nobility and men of quality, where a higher
tariff was charged, and where much wine and
good was drunk. Here in this locality, which
had long become the recognized rendezvous of
most of the wits and men of parts, the players
had their homes. Booth and Wilks had rendered Bow Street sacred in the memory of play-
goers ; and in this same street the ponderous
Quin lived at this date. Betterton had resided
in Russell Street, where Ryan now had his

home ; Colley Cibber dwelt in Charles Street, Macklin in St. James's Street, Mrs. Pritchard in Craven Street, Kitty Clive in Southampton Row, whilst the less famous actors and actresses lodged in the smaller streets branching from the Garden. They therefore met each other continually, and lived in a state of pleasant and friendly intercourse. Moreover, they could at less than an hour's notice be mustered together for rehearsal, in case a sudden change in a play-bill required the introduction of a fresh piece.

But it was not the players alone who flocked together in those days ; members of other callings and professions were apt to congregate in one spot likewise. Barristers and lawyers dwelt mostly in the Inns of Court, or about Westminster Hall ; whilst the merchants and bankers lived in their warehouses or counting-houses in the city, — few of them, and these only of the wealthiest, venturing to approach the West-end so near as Hatton Garden. Round Clare Market the butchers mustered in vast numbers. These brawny fellows were staunch friends of the players, to whom they were ever willing to give their services on occasions when disputes arose between them and the town, as was not infrequently the case ; and on nights when young

men of fashion, or gentlemen of the Inns of
Court, or the 'prentices bold, threatened a riot
in the playhouse on account of some supposed
offence given them by manager or actor, or
were determined on condemning an author's
play unheard, the timely appearance of such
formidable critics, stationed in various parts of
the house, made a due impression upon the
nerves of the would-be rioters.

The laws which held sway relative to the
playhouses were curious, but in some ways excellent, being of quite a different complexion
from those which obtain now-a-days. None
but persons of rank, quality, or fortune ever
presumed to sit in a box ; nor did a man ever
enter one with his head covered. The boxes
were moreover sacred to virtue and decorum,
except two or three on each side of the house,
which were specially set aside for the women
of the town. These were therefore visited by
men at the peril of their characters. No indifferent or vulgar person frequented the pit,
which was occupied by men of letters or wit,
by students of the Inns of Court, barristers, or
young merchants of rising eminence, all of whom
were supposed to be well read in polite litera-
ture, and learned in dramatic lore. There judgments were therefore considered worthy of vast

regard, as being dictated by experience, taste,
and learning. The players, as a consequence,
courted their good opinions in preference to
those of the occupants of any other part of the
house. When the play was over the critics began to talk, mustering in knots in the lobbies of
the theatre, or in the coffee-houses, — especially
the Bedford, — where they delivered judgments
according to their lights, which were received
by the town without dissent.

On nights when some attraction brought a
vast crowd to the house, an amphitheatre was
reared at the back of the stage, where presently
the spectators sat row upon row until the heads
of those seated in high places touched the theatrical clouds. When this was filled, groups of ill-
dressed lads sat in front of it, three or four rows
deep ; otherwise those behind could not have
seen, and a riot would have ensued. Nor was
this all ; round the single entrance-door at each
side, the young gentlemen of fashion crowded
in numbers, as this position gave them a delightful opportunity of displaying their handsomely
dressed persons to the best advantage. Here
they diverted themselves by staring, talking to
each other across the stage during the performance, making audible and not very complimentary comments on the actors, or such

people in the pit as attracted their notice and served as a butt for their wit. Such conduct was generally resented by the galleries, when the angry gods, in their just wrath, rained down on them showers of half-sucked oranges, half-eaten pippins, and unsound apples, to the infinite terror of those who sat in the pit and boxes.

The disadvantage under which this custom placed the poor players can scarcely be conceived. 'On a crowded night a performer could not step his foot with safety,' says Tate Wilkinson, ' lest he should thereby nurt or offend, or be thrown down amongst scores of idle, tipsy apprentices.' Amongst such a crowd would some charming Juliet be discovered in the tomb scene of ' Romeo and Juliet,' arrayed in a full white satin dress with large hoop, then considered indispensable to the proper costume of this love-sick maiden ; and with such a throng surrounding her bed would Desdemona bid her last farewell to the murderous Moor.

Sometimes, whilst the stage was so crowded, situations and scenes occurred in plays undreamt of by their authors. For instance, on one occasion, whilst an actor named Holland was playing Hamlet to a thronged house for his benefit, a ridiculous incident happened. When

the ghost, with some difficult and many audible
apologies, elbowed his way through the beaux
and appeared to this gentleman, his hat flew off
his head ; this being the recognised mode of
conveying a hint that his hair stood on end, and
of expressing fright generally. Presently, as
he complained that the air bit shrewdly, and
was very cold, a stout old lady with a com-
passionate heart and a red cloak stepped down
unseen by him, from her seat in the amphitheatre, picked up his hat, and coming behind
him, placed it on his head, when poor Hamlet
started in real terror. The house burst into
roars of laughter, the ghost turned and fled, and
Hamlet, after a moment's hesitation, followed
him amidst ringing cheers. On another night
it happened that a certain noble earl, during the
murder scene in Macbeth, lounged across the
stage in order to chat with a friend of his whom
he spied at the other side. Rich, the manager,
duly incensed, declared he would never admit
him on the stage again ; to which the noble
lord replied by giving him a blow in the face,
which was duly returned by Rich, when a fra-
cas commenced that extended itself to the whole
house. Indeed, this custom of crowding the
stage continued until 1762, when Garrick finally
abolished it, to the vast indignation of the audi-

SAMUEL JOHNSON, L. L. D.

ence and performers, — the former regarding it as an infringement on their rights, the latter as an injustice because of the decrease in the receipts of their benefits which ensued.

There were likewise unwritten laws regarding dress at this period, which were strictly adhered to, — the merchant being recognisable by his broadcloth and worsted hose, from the man of quality habited in velvet, satin, and silk. Moreover, those living at a distance of sixty or a hundred miles from the capital scarce ever ventured to make the journey to town ; but when they did, the countryman was at once known by his suit of light grey or drab cloth, his slouched hat, and uncurled hair.

It was only a couple of years before the Woffington's arrival that Samuel Johnson, in company with young Davy Garrick, had travelled up to London to seek his fortune, — when the philosopher in embryo had dined at the Pine Apple, in New Street, on a cut of meat for which he paid sixpence, and bread a penny ; or had in sadder times gone breadless by day and bedless by night, wandering wearily when all the world was asleep, in company with Richard Savage, poet and vagabond, round lonely squares and through deserted streets, silent save for the watchman's single-noted call or the striking of

many-toned clocks heard from towers and steeples lost in darkness, until with the dawn of a
new day fresh hopes were born within them.
But now Johnson, who has commenced to make
way, might be seen in one of the boxes of the
Fountain Tavern in the Strand, reading with
rumbling voice the ponderous speeches of his
tragedy ' Irene ' to Mr. Peter Garrick, or saun-
tering on ' clean shirt day ' to Salisbury Court
to visit Mr. Samuel Richardson the printer, then
unknown to fame ; or to carry copy to the
editor of the ' Gentleman's Magazine,' Mr. Edward Cave, of St. John's Gate, — a spot which
Johnson first ' beheld with reverence,' as the
source from which so much polite knowledge
sprang. Cave, a rough, gruff fellow enough,
who possessed a warm heart, was surrounded
by a crowd of hack writers, anxious to pen a
sonnet or satire, essay or article, at the nod
of their great chief. As an intellectual luxury,
he had promised Johnson a sight of the mighty
geniuses who presided over the fortunes of his
magazine, and subsequently introduced him to
them as they sat among the clouds, not of
Olympus, but of tobacco-smoke ascending from
their pipes in an ale-house in Clerkenwell.

Fielding, who had not at this time written a
line of his novels, but who was of good repute

E. CAVE.

as a dramatist, might be seen loitering in the
shop of his brother playwright, Robert Dodsley,
who had once been a footman in the Lowther
family, and had now become a poet, dramatist,
and publisher.

' You know how decent, humble, inoffensive
a creature Dodsley is, — how little apt to forget or disguise his having been a footman,'
writes Horace Walpole the magnificent. The
Muses, it would seem, had visited the worthy
Dodsley whilst he wore the shoulder-knot, and
the first volume of his poems was very appropriately entitled, 'The Muse in Livery.' These
verses were fortunate enough to attract the
attention of Pope, who, as the saying is, took
him by the hand and established him as a bookseller. In turn, Dodsley was one of the first
practically to recognise Johnson's worth as a
poet by giving him ten guineas for ' London,
a Poem in imitation of the third Satire of
Juvenal ; ' which ' happy offspring of his muse '
had previously gone the rounds of the book-
sellers and had been rejected by them. He
had likewise helped Johnson by giving him a
guinea now and then for paragraphs written for
the ' London Chronicle ' at a time when guineas
were most welcome guests to the philosopher's
palm.

In this pleasant shop, situated in Pall Mall, might be seen many of the celebrities of the day, — amongst others a thin-faced, shrunken-limbed little gentleman, slightly bent, and clad in sober black, who was no other than Mr. Pope of Twickenham. Here also came for many an hour's pleasant gossip a remarkable-looking man, pale-faced and with thoughtful eyes, — Edward Young, who had not then written his ' Night Thoughts,' but who had given Drury Lane a couple of tragedies which met with but little appreciation. And with him occasionally came a young man, a doctor's apprentice, — Tobias George Smollett, who eight years later was to become famous as the author of ' The Adventures of Roderick Random,' but who at this period, when he came to take a friendly pinch of snuff from Dodsley's box, and listen to the polite conversation of the men of parts who visited him, had merely written a tragedy which had been rejected by the managers of the Drury Lane and Covent Garden playhouses. Here too came young Mr. Arne, the upholsterer's son, — the brother of the frail and beautiful actress, Susanna Maria Cibber. Mr. Arne, a slight, trim man, light of foot and easy of carriage, who dressed in black velvet even in the dog-days, posed as a wit and a scholar, and had

SMOLLET.

just then distinguished himself by setting Milton's 'Comus' to music.

Peg Woffington and her lover arrived in the early part of the summer, when the theatrical season proper was almost over, and the actors and actresses were taking their annual benefits. At Drury Lane Mr. Quin was playing Julius Cæsar, ' with the death of Brutus and Cassius,' followed by the ' Virgin Unmasked,' in which saucy Kitty Clive played one of her favorite characters, — Miss Lucy. At Covent Garden ' The Rehearsal ' was being played for Mr. Cibber's benefit, with ' an epilogue written by Jo. Haines, comedian, of facetious memory, to be spoken by Mr. Cibber riding on an ass, followed by a hornpipe by a gentleman in the character of a sailor.' A pantomime entertainment, rejoicing in the suggestive title of ' The Columbine Courtezan,' was given nightly at Punch's Theatre, adjoining the Tennis Court in St. James's Street ; and instead of the usual operatic performances at the Haymarket Theatre, assemblies were held weekly, ' to commence at nine, and no sooner,' to which the gay part of the town flocked in large numbers.

Now that the long evenings and warm nights were at hand, the Marylebone Gardens threw wide their gates and gave entertainments of

music, when 'the nobility and gentry are admitted for sixpence each,' and Vauxhall put
forth all its gay allurements.

On these calm bright evenings in early summer the placid Thames was crowded by boats
and barges hung with bright bunting and laden
with gay companies of citizens on their way to
Vauxhall Gardens, which had then no rival, —
Ranelagh not being opened till April, 1742. In
the far-stretching gardens of Vauxhall were
woods, open swards, picturesque vistas, tents,
booths, and a platform for dancers; all of which
were at night 'made illustrious by a thousand
lights finely disposed.' In the glades, under
the shade of spreading trees, walked gentlemen
in silken hose and silver-buckled shoes, — their
rich-coloured velvet coats distended in the skirts
by cane or buckram, their padded breasts covered by bright-hued satin waistcoats, wide-flapped
and embroidered with gold or silver lace, their
jewelled hands half-covered by point-lace ruffles
smelling of orange-water, their powdered wigs
surmounted by three-cornered hats; and by
their sides walked ladies of quality, powdered
and patched, high-heeled, low-bodiced, and
wide-skirted. In the pavilions at either side
of the grove, which were divided into different departments, and adorned by pictures and

VIEW OF RANELAGH.

portraits by Hayman, from designs by Hogarth himself, sat various companies, not only of men and women of quality, but of goodly citizens in worsted hose and square-toed shoes and coats of honest broadcloth, who, with their buxom spouses and families, enjoyed themselves merrily enough ; for here, as Boswell says, 'was good eating and drinking for those who chose to purchase that regale.'

In the centre of the grove stood a vast orchestra, where bands played and 'concerts of musick' were given nightly ; and at either side of which stood statues of Mr. Handel as Orpheus playing the lyre — Roubiliac's first work in England — and of John Milton, the latter being cast in lead and painted stone-colour. Vauxhall had been opened by Mr. Thomas Tyres, a man who had been bred to the law, which he soon forsook ; for, having a vivacious temper and an eccentric mind, he ' ran about the world with a pleasant carelessness, amusing everybody,' as Johnson's biographer says. In opening Vauxhall Gardens, Tyres stated in his advertisements that he was ' merely ambitious of obliging the polite and worthy part of the town,' and charged a shilling simply ' to keep away such as were not fit to mix with those persons of quality, ladies and gentlemen,

and others,' who should honour him with their
company.

The gardens, from the convenience they afforded, soon became, as may be readily supposed, remarkable as a place of intrigue, — a
fact that did not in the least prevent others bent
on more innocent enjoyment from frequenting
them. To the diversions called *Ridotti al Fresco*,
given here, most of the company went, wearing
masks and dominos, and wrapping their figures
in ample cloaks, lawyer's gowns, and such arti-
cles of apparel as served for disguise. These
ridotti commenced at about eight o'clock in the
evening, and ended usually at four in the morning. They were extremely popular; and so prodigious a number of coaches and chairs crossed
Westminster Bridge *en route* for the gardens
from the polite part of the town, on nights
when a *ridotto* was held, that an attempt to
cross that thoroughfare oftentimes proved dangerous to limb and life. In the vicinity of
Vauxhall. order was sought to be preserved by
a hundred soldiers ; whilst the way from there
to town was patrolled by stout fellows well
armed, and paid by Tyres to protect the prop-
erties and lives of his patrons.

Horace Walpole pleasantly discourses of a
journey he made to Vauxhall in company with

Lady Caroline Petersham and Miss Ashe, with
whom, indeed, her ladyship had broke but a
little while before, but again took under her
protection upon the assurance of Miss Ashe
that she 'was as good as married' to Mr.
Wortley Montagu, Lady Mary's son, — a gentleman alike remarkable for the number of his
amours and his snuff-boxes.   When Walpole
arrived, he found the ladies 'had just finished
their last layer of red, and looked as handsome
as crimson could make them.'   The party also
numbered Lord March, Harry Vane, the Duke
of Kingston, pretty Miss Beauclerc, and Miss
Sparre.   As they sauntered down the Mall, a
merry group of bright-coloured ladies and powdered and perfumed gentlemen, Lady Caroline
met her lord, who strode by them on the outside and repassed them again without a word.
At the end of the Mall my lady called him, but
he would not hear ; when she gave a familiar
spring, and between laughing and confusion
called out to him, ' My lord, my lord !   Why,
you don't see us !'   Then the remainder of the
party advanced, feeling somewhat awkward and
anxious, for my lord did not love his lady ; and
Lady Caroline said, ' Do you go with us, or
are you going anywhere else ? '   To which her
lord and master made answer, ' I don't go with

you, I am going somewhere else!' and quickly
marched away. Not the less merry for his
departure, they got into a barge, a boat with a
company playing French horns attending them
as they floated down the tide. When they
debarked, whom should they meet but my lord
Granby, who reeled out of Jenny's Whim — a
tavern at the end of the wooden bridge at Chel-
sea — as drunk as may be, and who of course
accompanied them on their merry way; when
he took occasion to propose to Miss Sparre
that they should shut themselves up for three
weeks merely to rail at the world. Then they
entered the Gardens and selected a box, in
front of which Lady Caroline sat, looking dan-
gerously handsome. Learning that my lord
Orford was in a neighbouring box, she sent for
him to mince chickens ; when seven of these
unhappy fowls were minced into a china dish,
which her hospitable ladyship stewed over a
lamp with three pats of butter and a flagon of
water, stirring and rattling and laughing till the
company expected to have the dish about their
ears every moment. My lady had brought Betty,
the famous fruit-girl, who in her turn brought
hampers of strawberries and cherries; and Betty
waited on this excellent company, and then sat
down at a little table beside them and enjoyed

her share of the good things of this life. Such
jokes and puns and repartee — sometimes a little
broad, it is true — never were heard ; such wit
fell from their lips, such laughter rippled all
round them, that they soon had the whole attention of the garden, and crowds gathered
about their box, till Harry Vane took up a
bumper and drank their healths, and then proceeded to treat them with greater freedom, —
when they dispersed.

Mention of Vauxhall is continually made in
the newspapers of the day, in connection with
the announcements of its *fêtes*, the people who
had visited it, and sometimes with strange advertisements, — one of which, strongly illustrative of the times, runs : ' Lost in the dark walk
at Vauxhall last week, two female reputations ;
one had a small speck, on account of some
dirt previously thrown at it, the other never
soiled. Whoever will bring them back to their
owners shall receive five thousand pounds, with
thanks.'

CHAPTER III.

A Faithless Lover. — Fortune-hunting. — News of a Marriage. — Hatred and Vengeance. — Peg Woffington's Plot. — Young Mr. Adair. — The Ridotto at Vauxhall Gardens. — Miss Dallaway and her Friends. — A Scene. — Reproaches. — A Lover's Departure.

SUCH was London town when Peg Woffington and young Taaffe took up their residence in York Street, Covent Garden. For a few brief months all went well with them ; the actress was delighted with the infinite attractions and novelties of the capital, and her lover rejoiced that she was happy.

But by degrees, slow but deadly sure, came the inevitable reaction of a passion not founded on unselfish affection ; and the man who had sworn that he loved her more than life itself, and that his love for her would outlive his life, already grew cold in his ardour. For days and weeks he was absent from her side. But she who had given him her heart loved him still, and was loath to admit that her affection was no longer returned ; and by all those charming arts which the intuition of a woman of fine feelings teaches her to employ in inspiring or retaining a love that is dear to her, she strove to win him back once more. For a time it seemed as if she had succeeded ; to his carelessness ensued a tenderness that had in it something of self-reproach. At last there came a day when he announced that urgent business affairs in connection with his property obliged him to leave town for Ireland, but he hoped to return in three weeks at the latest. And then followed many protestations of affection, which even she felt came rather from the lips than from the heart ; for the old light was missing from his sea-blue eyes, and the sound of his voice rang false.

He had scarcely gone a week when it reached her ears that he had been playing her false, — that he had been wooing a young lady of quality and fortune, named Miss Dallaway, who was heiress to considerable wealth. Moreover, his attentions to this young lady had proved so agreeable that she had promised to wed him on his return to town. At this news the Woffington was by turns astonished, incredulous, and furious; but recovering from the first condition, she took pains to ascertain that the rumour was undoubtedly true. Then the scales fell from her eyes, and she saw that the idol she had blindly worshipped had not a heart of gold, as she had foolishly imagined, but of base clay, made very much after the pattern of the rest of mankind. She was not jealous of the woman he had asked to marry him, probably for the sake of her money; but she was heart-sore for loss of his love, indignant at the deception practised on her, and humiliated at the prospect of being flung aside at the mere dictates of his caprice and convenience. Brooding over her wrongs, all her love for him turned to hatred and contempt; she was a woman scorned, and she was determined to have vengeance.

It was not until she had thought for long and sorrowful days that she at last hit upon a plan of obtaining her vengeance; but this, when once determined on, she, with the impetuous spirit which was so strong a trait of her character, did not hesitate to carry out. Knowing the name of the lady to whom her lover had proposed marriage, it was a matter of but slight difficulty to become acquainted with her by sight; for, being a woman of quality and fashion, she attended all the polite assemblies and entertainments of the town. The next step that the Woffington resolved on was to meet her, obtain an introduction to her, and reveal to her that the man she had promised to wed was the lover

of an Irish actress. Thoughts of the sore pain
and deep humiliation which this might cause
Miss Dallaway did not prevent the Woffington
from carrying out her plans ; this woman of
fashion could not love him as she, the Woffington, had loved him, — with all the depth and
force of her demonstrative Celtic nature, quick,
subtle, and passionate ; and if she had suffered
from his perfidy, why not this other woman
likewise ? It was but just! She must strike at
him, though her shaft pierced another heart.

Remembering how successfully she had played
the part of Sir Harry Wildair on the stage, she
now resolved, in order to carry out her plans
more successfully, to act the part of a young
man of fashion in real life ; and assuming male
attire, she so successfully disguised herself that
even those who had seen her take the part in
the Dublin theatre could not recognize her as
Mr. Adair, a young Irishman of family and fortune,— the name and character she now assumed.
Attired in silken hose and satin breeches, with
broidered waistcoat and wide-flapped coat, powdered, painted, and bewigged, she sallied forth
upon the town, a perfect specimen of the impertinent, dainty, and effeminate coxcombs of
the period. Everywhere Miss Dallaway went,
the Woffington was, if possible, present, — in

the park before dinner, where the lady was sure
to take the air; in the theatre at night, where
the lady sat in her box; and to such assemblies
as were open to the public for payment, where
the lady was most likely to attend.　Moreover,
the Woffington always took care that Miss Dallaway should notice her appearance, and occasionally ventured to give such signs of admiration
and indications of a smitten heart as were per-
missible by look and gesture.

But all the while the Woffington found it
impossible to obtain the desired introduction,
without which she dared not, in her character
as a gallant, address the lady.　At length fate
granted her desire one night, when they were
present at a public *ridotto* in Vauxhall Gardens.
When the Woffington, otherwise Mr. Adair,
entered the grounds, the scene which presented
itself was one of vast brilliancy and gaiety.　In
the orchestra a full band was discoursing the
liveliest airs imaginable; coloured lamps glit-
tered amidst the thick-leaved branches of oak
and linden that formed an arch-like roof above
the central walk of the grove; the pavilions
were crowded with brightly clad figures; dancers glided to and fro upon the platform; laughter rang in the air; and everywhere were men
and women in masks, dominos, uniforms, or

fancy costumes, busy in the pursuit of enjoyment, and all as merry as might be.

Amongst those Mr. Adair walked with a swaggering gait, swinging his gold-knobbed clouded cane with its great bunch of silken tassels to and fro, as if his heart were as light as a feather, — a smile on his lips, a civil speech on his tongue, a glitter in his eye that might indicate love or mischief. At last he caught sight of the figure for which he had been diligently in search. Surrounded by a group of friends, Miss Dallaway sat under a tree, watching the crowds pass and repass, now and then making some comment which showed she was not devoid of wit. Approaching the little knot with the easiest and most careless air in the world, Mr. Adair recognized at a glance a certain man of quality with whom he had during the week exchanged civilities whilst dining at the more select ordinary of the Bedford, and with whom on one occasion he had cracked a bottle of port. Advancing to him, he assumed his most courteous air, made a bow which carried its credentials for good breeding in its every movement, and spoke a vastly civil speech. The man of quality was not behindhand in courtesy, and presently young Adair making a polite reference to Miss Dallaway, the man of quality offered to introduce his new friend to her.

' For,' said he, 'you must know the young lady has a partiality for your country, having given the strongest possible proof of it by consenting to wed one of your genial-hearted race.'

' Indeed,' said Mr. Adair. ' The young lady confers an honour on us all by her choice, — all the more so from her condescending to overlook the worth and parts of those by whom she is at present surrounded.'

When the elaborate bows which succeeded this speech were made, and the gentlemen had assumed their erect figures once more, Mr. Adair was presented to Miss Dallaway, — a young gentlewoman of scarcely more than eighteen summers, beautiful in features, dazzlingly fair, blue-eyed, and with an expression of innocence and trust that quickly won its way to the heart. At the introduction, Mr. Adair slowly removed his hat, and placing it, with a gesture perfect in gracefulness, over the region of his heart, bowed almost to the ground ; whilst the lady, first rising from her seat, seemed gradually and gently to sink amidst billows of lace and satin as she curtesyed low in return.

' Madam,' said Mr. Adair, in a voice which,

FRONT OF OLD DRURY LANE THEATRE.

though a trifle harsh, had in its undertone a ring
which attracted its hearer, 'this day shall henceforth be reckoned amongst the happiest in my
life.'

' Sir,' said the lady, ' you are in truth vastly
polite ; ' and raising her eyes to his, she encountered a glance the fascination of which few
men had found it possible to resist.

' Madam,' said this pretty gentleman, ' when
the truth is spoken concerning you, it must ever
seem polite ; for with such a theme, no tongue
could discourse inelegantly.'

The lady bowed once more, and opened her
jewelled fan, which she raised to her face in order to conceal the smile of pleasure that played
about her lips.

' You have a knack, sir,' she said, ' of turning pretty compliments.'

' Yes, madam,' quoth he, ' when inspired by
beauty and worth ; for compliments are the due
tributes to such qualities.' And so saying, the
gallant gentleman tapped a tiny gold box, helped
himself with an air of satisfaction to snuff, and
taking out his daintily scented handkerchief,
lightly brushed a few grains which had fallen on
the costly lace of his ruffles.

By degrees Miss Dallaway's friends gave way
to the new-comer, whose easy grace and vast

1. — 4

courtesy seemed to find ready favour in her
eyes. Mr. Adair, seeing his advantage, quickly
followed it up ; he was anxious to speak to her
in a more sequestered spot, in order to expose
the villainy of the man she had promised to
wed. Therefore he said to her, as soon as the
opportunity offered, —

' The crowd here to-night is prodigious,
madam ; in faith, we have around us a mixed
lot. You will find it more agreeable in the
grove, I have no doubt ; may I do myself the
honour of offering you my arm ? '

And so saying, he led the way down the central walk of the grove, with its star-like lights
and its fragrant odours. By degrees, and as
it seemed by accident, they outstepped their
friends ; for the crowd through which they
moved being great, they were soon separated
from her,—an advantage which was quickly
followed up by the young gentleman proposing
that they should turn down one of the paths to
the right, inasmuch that it was far more agreeable by reason of its silence and seclusion.

' I believe, sir, by your conversation, that
you live in town,' said the lady, laying her hand
on his arm as lightly as might be.

' At present, yes, madam,' says he ; ' I have,
however, been here but a few short months,

having arrived in the spring from — from one
of the universities.'

'Young gentlemen are taught many things
there,' says she.

'Yes, madam,' replies he, with a wicked
smile; 'in the one from which I came they
learned many things — from me.'

'From you, sir!' stealing a glance at him.

'That is, I taught them some very pretty
manners; I have always been famed for my
manners.'

'Of that I have no doubt, sir,' replied the
lady.

'But alas! madam,' the gentleman said with
a sigh, 'I find that I have come to town too
late.'

He felt as if he were playing a part; the
habit of acting, difficult to lay aside even in
serious moments, was now strong upon him;
the gardens with their lights and music were
but a stage, the surroundings but theatrical
accessories, and the purport for which he had
donned this disguise and sallied forth upon the
town for the last week but the plot of a comedy.
And yet it was all real, terribly real; and under
the bravery of that broidered satin waistcoat
beat a woman's heart that was sick from grief,
yet strong for revenge.

' Too late ?　May I venture to inquire why you say so ? ' said Miss Dallaway.

'If I only dared to tell her,' said the gentleman, in that undertone called on the stage an aside, which, though quite audible, is supposed to be unheard.　Then he added in a louder though more desponding tone, ' Too late, madam, to secure my own happiness.'

' How do you mean?' queried Miss Dallaway, who seemed to conceive a sudden interest in the cause of his distress.

' When I came to town,' said he, lifting his eyes to hers and catching a look of pleasure which promised a deeper concern in his affairs, ' I heard the name of Miss Dallaway on every tongue.　In the coffee-houses it was spoken with respectful admiration, in all polite assemblies with unmeasured praise.　Everywhere her beauties and qualities were vastly lauded, until I grew impatient to see the object of such general esteem.　But when at last good fortune permitted me to see her, — when I saw you, madam, I knew that all I had heard had not done justice to your perfections ; I saw that your merits were as far superior to the compliments which every tongue had uttered as glorious day is to the darkness of night, as heaven itself is to this poor earth.'

'Oh, sir,' said the lady, blushing, 'you over-whelm me.'

'Nay, madam,' said the gallant, 'I speak but the naked truth. But with the knowledge of your perfections came also the news that you had given your love, your life, to the keeping of one who had been happy enough to find favour in your eyes.'

'That is true, sir,' said the lady, as if the fact had been suddenly recalled to her, and recalled without pleasure; 'he — he is a gentleman of worth,' she added.

'If he were indeed one likely to render you happy, madam,' said the gallant, 'I would never have sought this interview to-night.'

'What do you mean, sir?' said Miss Dalla-way, with a change of tone that indicated both surprise and displeasure.

'I mean,' he answered boldly, 'that he is unworthy of your esteem and love; that in fact, madam, he is a worthless fellow and a profligate.'

'It is false!' she said indignantly, removing her hand from her companion's arm. 'This is a charge trumped up to blacken his character in my eyes, — an unworthy trick to ingratiate yourself in my favour; but, clever as you are, sir, it shall not succeed.'

'Upon my honour, madam, it is true,' said Mr. Adair, very quietly. 'I see you love him too, and I grieve indeed to pain you, — in truth I do ; but this gentleman is well known, as I have recently learned, for his gallantries. Nay, bear with me whilst I tell you that even while he made love to you from mercenary motives, he was carrying on an affair with an actress whom he brought to town from Ireland.'

'An actress ?' she gasped, pale now, and trembling all over. Then, the colour coming back into her cheeks, she cried out, ' I 'll not believe it ; it cannot be possible that the man who swore he loved me — loved me better than all the world besides, loved me for myself alone — is false to me. Take back your words ; say they are untrue, the trick of a rival in a war of love ; or ' (with a change of tone no longer pleading but commanding) ' produce me proof that your words are true.'

' Madam,' said the Woffington, — for it was no longer the man of fashion but the woman who now spoke, — ' I cannot take back my words ; but as it may be well for you to know this man, I will show you proof that what I have said is true ; ' and she drew out a bundle of letters, some of them of recent date, some

of them well worn because often read. ' You
know the writing ? '

The young lady fixed her eyes on them for a
second, and nodded her head.

' Then read them,' said the Woffington.

In her haste, Miss Dallaway almost tore the
squarely folded sheets of paper bearing Taaffe's
seal and his characters addressed to Mrs. Mar-
garet Woffington, and read line after line that
spoke of love and faithfulness for this actress,
until the letters seemed to burn themselves into
her brain ; then the music of the band fell
fainter and fainter on her ears, her head swam,
and with a low cry she tottered forward, and
would have fallen but that Peg Woffington
caught her in her outstretched arms. The place
was quite solitary ; no one had witnessed this
scene. With an effort Peg Woffington lifted
the insensible girl to a bench close by, fanned
her face and chaffed her hands.

' Poor girl,' she said, ' I did not think she
loved him so ! What fools we women are ! '
Tears sprang into her eyes, and bending down
her head, she kissed the girl's forehead with
tenderness. ' Did you know me, you would
shrink from the touch of my lips,' she said, almost in a whisper ; and again she kissed her
with the love of a sister.

In a little while the young lady opened her eyes, and looking round her, remembered all.

' My child,' said the Woffington, tenderly, forgetting completely the character she assumed, ' I have caused you some pain ; but from suffering good often springs. It is best that you should know the man to whom you were about to trust the happiness of your whole life as he really is. When next a man pleads to you, have more care regarding his character, before you give him the treasure of your love.'

' You have saved me,' said the girl. ' I loved him, and now — now — '

' You see he is unworthy of you. My task has been, after all, an ungracious one ; and when I undertook it I had no thought for the trouble it might bring you. Forgive me.'

'Then it was not to save me you told me this ? ' said Miss Dallaway, wonderingly.

' No ; it was to punish him for his deception to — to one very near to me,' said the Woffington. Her cheeks were burning.

' In any case I owe you thanks,' said the young lady, while tears almost choked her voice. ' Your words are kind ; surely, ah ! surely your heart must be good.'

' Good ? If you knew me you would not say so,' said the Woffington. Then she hesitated

just for a second ; longing, in obedience to
some sudden impulse, to throw off the character
she had assumed and reveal herself, yet fearing
to lose the regard which she had gained, and
dreading the dislike and distrust which she knew
her name must call up. Suddenly resuming her
former air of a coxcomb, she therefore laughed
airily and said, ' Madam, believe me, I am no
better than my neighbours.'

Miss Dallaway rose up, puzzled by the con-
tradictions in manner and tone which this young
man's action betrayed.

' Let us seek my friends,' she said. ' I 'm
sure they have missed me.'

She held out her hand, which the Woffington
took in both of hers, and raised it to her lips,
not with affected gallantry, but in honest pity.
Then arm in arm, and without exchanging
another word, they went forth amongst the
crowd.

The first light of a summer day had crept into
the sky before the Woffington reached her lodgings in York Street, Covent Garden. In obedience to the loud summons of one of her
chairmen, the door was quickly opened, not by
a servant, but by her lover, who had just returned. She started for a moment in surprise ;
then getting out of her chair, she quickly passed

him and entered the house, leaving him to
wrangle with the chairmen. Passing into the
sitting-room, she flung off her dainty gold-laced
hat and powdered wig, loosened her cravat,
undid her sword, cast it from her on the floor
impatiently, and then sat down in a great chair
to await his coming. Her mood had changed.
The manner of the man about town had vanished
completely; the air of reckless audacity had
given place to the weariness of reaction; the
scene in which she had so cleverly enacted a
part, now affected her in an unlooked-for degree,
and filled her with bitter self-reproach.

'Well, Peggy,' said Taaffe, entering the room
with a blithe air, 'have you no word of welcome
for me, after coming back to you four days
sooner than I expected?'

'I am tired,' she answered, shortly, without
looking at him.

Her face was white and haggard seen by this
early light; there was a dangerous glitter in her
dark eyes, a defiant air in her bearing.

'Ah, I see,' said he, with a short laugh.
'You have been out amusing yourself at your old
stage tricks again, and donning the breeches.'

Coming over to where she was, he sat down
beside her, and stretched out his arms as if to
caress her, with such tenderness as was his

General View *of* COVENT GARDEN MARKET,
LONDON .

wont in the first days of their courtship. The same light was in his sea-blue eyes, the same smile on his lips which had first dazzled her, filled her heart with a torrent of happiness, and made her weigh the world light in the balance of his love. But now she saw only the weakness, deception, and cruelty of his nature reflected in his eyes and playing on his lips, and she shrank from him.

' Don't touch me,' she said, in a tone such as he had never heard her use before. He did not dare to disobey her.

' Why,' said he, ' it 's in mighty bad temper you are ; you don't seem to have got much diversion out of your night.'

' I have got none,' she answered him, briefly.

' It 's sorry I am for it,' he said, conciliatingly. ' And may I ask where you have been ? '

' You may, for I intended telling you. Though I may act many parts, I cannot play the hypocrite like you.' This time she looked him in the face.

' What the devil do you mean by that civil speech ? ' asked the gentleman, beginning to comprehend her humour.

' I mean,' she answered, ' that I have seen Miss Dallaway, the woman you promised to marry, and I have told her all.'

'Good God!' cried he, nervously grasping hold of his chair. 'Is this a part of your play-acting, or is it true? Answer me at once —'

'It is true,' she replied, unflinchingly meeting the look of horror that crept into his face.

'You are a devil!' he almost hissed from between his clenched teeth.

'I am a woman,' she said, rising to her feet, and throwing back her finely turned head with so sudden a gesture that her long black hair fell in a lustrous shower upon her shoulders, — 'I am a woman, and you have deceived me. I loved you with all my heart, and you played me false. You swore fidelity to me, and then left me to whisper the same words in the ear of another dupe of your flattering speeches and soft ways. All the love I once bore you turned to hate, and I determined to expose you as the liar and hypocrite that you are.'

Her eyes flashed, her breast heaved with passion, her face flushed with the crimson of indignation. She was beautiful; but the man before her thought only of the injury she had done him. His anger blinded him to the loveliness that had once fascinated him, and he rose up and cursed her.

'Tell me what you have done,' he gasped,

seeing it was better for him to know the worst
at once. 'What you have said to her.'

'I have told her that you are a profligate,'
she said, looking at him steadily. 'I have told
her that even whilst you spoke words of love to
her, you were carrying on an affair with — with
an actress you had brought with you from
Ireland.'

The words came as if wrenched from her.

'She will not believe you,' he said, catching
at some straw by which he might yet be saved.

'I have taken care that she shall. I have
shown her your letters to me,' she answered.

'Good God! I am undone,' he cried out in
despair. 'Do you know that you have ruined
me? My affairs are going to the devil. She
is an heiress; I was to have married her in a
couple of weeks, and her fortune would have
saved me. You have destroyed me.'

Woman like, she began to relent. He strode
up and down the room with uneven steps, his
face pale as death, his brows knitted in anger,
his lips twitching from the passion of his
despair.

'I only know,' she answered back, with
strongly imposed calmness, 'that you have deceived me. It was enough for me.'

'You — you are a tigress,' he replied, hoarse

with rage ; and snatching up his cloak and hat he rushed out of the room and out of the house without another word ; nay, even without once looking back at her.

For a moment she stood motionless, listening to the quick sound of his feet echoing down the lonely street in the early morning hour. Even then she knew that she would never again see this man whom she had loved so well, whom she, alas! yet loved, despite her wrongs and her rage. Even then she felt that time had turned over one of the brightest pages of her life, that something had gone from her existence which she could never again recover. Then a dull sense of misery and unutterable loneliness descended on her ; and with a passionate movement she flung herself on a couch, and burying her face in her hands, sobbed as if her heart were breaking.

CHAPTER IV.

John Rich, Manager of Covent Garden. — His First Pantomime. — His Treatment of Dramatic Authors. — The Woffington's Interview with Him. — Sensation in the Town. — Actors at Covent Garden. — Ryan's Tragedy in Real Life.— Theophilus Cibber. — Peg Woffington's First Appearance in London. — An Old-fashioned Comedy. — Surprise and Admiration of the Town. — Sir Harry Wildair. — All the Town in Love with Her.

PEG WOFFINGTON was not a woman to sit down idly, and break her heart because of a lover's perfidy. Naturally energetic, she delighted in work, and happily for her generation of play-goers, now resolved to offer her services for the coming season to John Rich, who had eight years previously built Covent Garden theatre, of which he was now manager. Rich was a prominent character in his day ; remarkable for his eccentricities, and famous as being the first to introduce that form of entertainment now known as pantomime into England. In common justice to his memory, it must be borne in mind that his productions were of a far more refined and intelligible order than these which obtain at the present day. His

first attempt in this direction was the representation of a story from Ovid's ' Metamorphoses,'
which, by the aid of magnificent scenes, glit-
tering habits, charming dances, together with
music and singing, he made wonderfully at-
tractive to the town. Between the acts of this
serious representation he interwove a comic
fable, which was chiefly founded on the courtship of his beautiful columbine and the heroic
harlequin, — a character it was the great delight
of his life to represent. In this performance a
variety of the most surprising adventures and
tricks were produced by the mere wave of a
magic wand : cottages and huts were trans-
formed into palaces all a-glitter with silver and
gold ; men and women were turned in the
twinkling of an eye into trees and stones ; vast
gardens sprung from the earth ; and such things
happened as had never before been witnessed
by the play-going world. The result was a
complete success.

Rich was the son of a gentleman, but was
wholly illiterate ; this being probably due to
some neglect in his education, for by the in-
vention of his pantomimes he proved himself
to be a man of imagination and ability. The
treatment of his harlequin likewise showed that
he possessed the innate refinement of good-

breeding. His 'Catching the Butterfly' was
declared by the chronicles of his times to be a
most wonderful performance ; whilst his harlequin, hatched from an egg by the heat of the
sun, proved such an attraction that crowds waited for admission under the piazza of Covent
Garden from mid-day, and threatened to break
down the doors of the playhouse if they were
not admitted at three o'clock, at least two hours
before the entertainment commenced. This
performance was said to be a masterpiece of
dumb show, for Rich's harlequin never uttered
a word; yet such was the power he exhibited by
his gestures and expressions, that he not only
provoked laughter, but drew tears. Jackson,
speaking of the last-mentioned pantomime, says
of Rich, or rather of the harlequin, 'from the
first chipping of the egg, his receiving of motion, his feeling of the ground. his standing up-
right, to his quick harlequin trip round the
empty shell, — through the whole progression,
every limb had its tongue, and every motion a
voice, which spoke with most miraculous organ
to the understandings and sensations of the
observers.'

Rich's success was such that his example was
quickly followed ; and Drury Lane and the
minor houses introduced harlequinades, in order

I. — 5

to draw full audiences.   So important, indeed,
did the character of harlequin become, that he
was played by such clever and accomplished
actors as Woodward, O'Brien, Yates, and even
Garrick himself, on an occasion when the regu-
lar harlequin of Goodman's Fields playhouse
was taken suddenly ill ; this being, of course,
before he attempted the part of Richard the
Third in the same theatre.   By degrees the
harlequinade became vulgarized, and we read of
one of those entertainments presented at the
last-mentioned house which greatly took the
town.   This was called ' A Hint to the Theatre,
or Merlin in Labour ; with the Birth, Adventures, Execution, and Restoration of Harlequin,
by Mr. Devoto.'   The bills announcing this
stated that, as the manager had put himself to
great expense in getting the machinery made
' to the neatest perfection,' he hoped to be
favoured with ' the company of the curious.'
Accordingly, the curious and others flocked to
witness the performance in great numbers.

Perhaps it was the success of his dumb shows
which helped Rich to cherish a fine contempt in
his managerial soul for his contemporary play-
writers, whom he sorely aggrieved.   When
these children of the muses sent him their manu-
scripts, Rich flung them into the deep drawer of

a cabinet, where they lay for months. Presently, when the aspirants for fame timidly approached him, and asked him, with bated breath, for tidings of their full-blooded tragedies or farcical comedies, the manager would coolly inform them he did not know which plays were theirs; but they might go to the deep drawer of the cabinet and take their choice, for he wanted none of them. This little peculiarity of his got him into trouble, on one occasion at least. It happened that a medical man, ' calling himself Sir John Hill,' left a manuscript play of his, entitled, ' Orpheus,' with Rich, or rather with that gentleman's maidservant. Of course it shared the fate, alas! common to its kind; the manager never untying even the outer covering. In due time Mr. Rich announced the performance at his theatre of a play called ' Orpheus,' which, ' though done by a different hand,' the doctor insisted on claiming as his property. Subsequently a war of words followed, in which the whole town took part. Then he who called himself Sir John Hill published his ' Orpheus,' in the preface of which he stated his case according to his lights. This was quickly followed by a pamphlet bearing the comprehensive title, ' Mr. Rich's answer to the many falsities and calumnies advanced by Mr. John Hill, Apothecary ; ' which in turn elicited another ' Answer to the many Plain and Notorious *Lyes* advanced by Mr. John Rich, Harlequin ; ' and so this paper war raged quite briskly for many months.

For all this, Rich was, like most of those following the same calling, a good-hearted fellow enough ; in testimony of which statement a story is told of his behaviour to a poor man who fell from the gallery to the pit of Covent Garden, whilst witnessing some strange escapades of the harlequin. When the man was picked up, his bones were found to be broken in many places ; learning which, Rich had him carefully tended, employing for the purpose the best medical skill of the town. A few months later the poor fellow came to thank the manager for his kindness, when Rich said to him in his most serious manner, —

' Well, my man, you must never try to come into the pit in that fashion again ; and to prevent it, I 'll give you free admission to that part of the house as long as I live.'

To the residence of John Rich, situated in the then highly fashionable quarter of Bloomsbury Square, the Woffington betook herself,

and demanded an interview with the eccentric
manager ; but as she refused to give her name,
she found this was no easy matter to obtain.
According to John Galt, she paid no less than
nineteen visits before she was admitted. At
last she told the servant to say Miss Woffington
desired to speak with Mr. Rich ; when the man
returned with a thousand civil speeches and
apologies, and informing her that his master
would see her at once, showed her into his
private apartment. Entering the room, she
found the manager lounging on a sofa, a book
in one hand, a china cup, from which he occasionally sipped tea, in another, whilst around
him were seven-and-twenty cats, engaged in
the various occupations of staring at him, lick-
ing his teacup, eating the toast from his
mouth, walking round his shoulders, and frisk-
ing about him with the freedom of long-standing
pets.

The fame of Peg Woffington's achievements
in the Dublin playhouse had crossed the Channel, and made the manager willing to entertain
her proposal of playing at his theatre during
the following season. A salary of nine pounds
a week was offered her, which she accepted
willingly enough, and an engagement was

then entered into, when it was decided that she should make her first bow to the English public in the following November, as Sylvia, in George Farquhar's comedy, 'The Recruiting Officer.'

The rumour that this new actress, who had the rare fortune to be appreciated in her own country, and whose beauty was, moreover, reputed to be little less than that of a goddess, was about to play at Covent Garden, made a vast sensation in the town. She was, on this her first appearance, to play the leading character, and to be supported by two actors who were popular favourites, Ryan and Theophilus Cibber, — players, both, who subsequently acted with her for years. Ryan, the son of an Irish tailor, had, when he and the century were in their teens, played in Macbeth with the famous Betterton ; on which most memorable occasion he, as Seyton, had worn a tremendous full-bottomed wig, which almost smothered him. From that day he had laboured with such effect in his profession, that Addison had selected him to play Marcus, in his great, long-winded tragedy of ' Cato ; ' and Garrick, in after years, confessed that this actor's ' Richard III.' was a performance after which he had shaped his own.

His fame as a tragedian was not indeed confined
to the stage, for he had killed his man in real
life, surrounded by such commonplace effects
as a tavern furnished.

It happened one summer evening, as early as
the year 1718. that after his performance in the
Lincoln's Inn Fields playhouse he had gone
to sup quietly at the Sun, in Long Acre ; and
for the purpose of being more at his ease, he
had taken off his sword, and placed it in the
window. But as fate would have it. scarce
had he laid by his weapon, when in struts,
with the most rakish air imaginable. a famous
bravado named Kelly, whose chief diversion it
was to pick quarrels with strangers, in taverns
and coffee-houses, and then fall upon them with
preconceived malice and wound them bodily,
he being an excellent swordsman. On the
present occasion, being flushed with wine and
full of bravery, he approached Ryan, who was
quietly sitting at a far table, and first daring
him to fight him, he subsequently made passes
at him which meant deadly harm ; the actor,
therefore, rushed for his sword. At this, Kelly
seemed mightily diverted, and made thrusts at
him afresh ; whereon Ryan, in self-protection,
skilfully ran a sword through the body of his

assailant, who in another second lay stark upon the tavern floor, his sword grasped tight in his stiff right hand, his life's blood oozing on the sand. The town was delighted beyond expression to get rid of this troublesome fellow, and Ryan in consequence rose in popular favour. Indeed, such a hold did he take on the public, that when subsequently he was set on in mistake whilst returning home late at night, and received a wound in the cheek that made his voice sound sharp and shrill, his audiences completely overlooked this defect, and never moved him from the warmth of their favour.

Theophilus Cibber, son of old Colley, who was to act the part of Plume in 'The Recruiting Officer' on the Woffington's first appearance, had made that character a special study, and had been instructed in it by his father. Theo Cibber, as he was most frequently called, had 'a person far from pleasing, and the features of his face were rather disgusting,' as David Erskine Baker, Esquire, quaintly informs us. Theophilus Cibber had from early in his career developed what was known as 'a fondness for indulgences;' in other words, he was a scapegrace of the first water, as will presently be seen. But

he had a good understanding, a quickness of
parts, a perfect knowledge of the characters he
represented, and a certain amount of vivacity
occasionally amounting to *effronterie*, which com-
bined to make him an actor agreeable to the
town. He had been, it may be noted, the origi-
nal George Barnwell in the tragedy of that
title.

Now this play preached a moral, which,
though a rare thing enough in those days, was
by no means acceptable to the public ; in consequence of which, it was usual to introduce an
epilogue at the end, which ridiculed, broadly of
course, all the virtuous and beautiful sentiments
gone before. To heighten the fun and give it a
sharper relish, this was spoken by Mrs. Cibber,
who, smartly and with little disguise, satirised
her husband's vices (for he had many, 't was
said) and excused her own, which were indeed
the common property of the town. To render
the occasion of Peg Woffington's first appearance the more important, Rich bespoke the
favour of the presence of Frederick, Prince of
Wales and his Princess ; and as His Royal
Highness was always anxious to be diverted, he
graciously promised to be present.

The play-bill announcing the performance ran
as follows : —

COVENT GARDEN.

By command of His Royal Highness the PRINCE OF
WALES.

By the Company of Comedians,
AT THE THEATRE ROYAL IN COVENT GARDEN,
This day will be presented a Comedy, call'd
THE RECRUITING OFFICER,
WRITTEN BY THE LATE MR. FARQUHAR.
The part of SYLVIA by MISS WOFFINGTON
(Being the first time of her performing on that Stage).
WITH DANCING
By MON. DESNOYER and SIGNORA BARBERINI,
ALSO
By MON. and MADEMOISELLE MECHEL
(The French Boy and Girl).
To which by command will be added a Tragi-Comi-
Pastoral Farce of Two Acts, call'd
THE WHAT D'YE CALL IT.
Box, 5s.; Pit, 3s.; First Gallery, 2s.; Upper Gallery, 1s.
To begin exactly at Six o'clock.

On the evening of the 6th of November,
1740, at the hour of six o'clock, a brilliant and
crowded audience had assembled in Covent
Garden Theatre. In the royal box, ' under a
canopy of scarlet silk, most richly adorned with

gold tissue and tassels of the same,' sat the
Prince and Princess of Wales ; and in the boxes
around them the gay and witty courtiers who
had turned their backs on St. James's, to frisk,
flatter, sparkle, and enjoy themselves in the
light of the rising sun, who never — alas for him
and them ! — reached the meridian of his power.
In the pit, as usual, sat the students of the Inns
of Court, the men about town, the young fellows from the Universities, with their periwigs,
swords, ruffles, and snuff-boxes ; glib compliments on their lips, merry twinkles in their eyes,
and much knowledge of stage affairs in their
heads, by which they would presently, over a
glass of wine, try this Irish actress, and pro-
nounce judgment upon her. Presently, when
the fiddles had played their last long-drawn
notes, and the candles forming the footlights
had been judiciously snuffed, up went the heavy
green curtain ; then a silence fell upon the
house, broken only by the fluttering of fans and
the snapping of snuff-box lids.

The ' Recruiting Officer,' a comedy in which
the Woffington's name is closely connected, and
in which she continued to divert the town for
years, had from its lively action, spirited dialogue, and rather broad fun, been long a standing favourite with playgoers.

Moreover, 't was said to be true to life, and indeed it gives an excellent picture of the manners and ways of the times. George Farquhar had been himself a recruiting officer at Shrewsbury, where the scene is laid, and where he wrote the play; and it was said he had drawn his own character in that of Captain Plume, 'a rakehelly officer,' who is the hero of the comedy. The heroine, Sylvia, daughter of worthy Justice Ballance, is a young gentlewoman full of dash and spirit, as may be gathered from the autobiographical details, with which, in the first act, she is kind enough to favour her cousin Melinda, who remarks that she, Sylvia, has the 'constitution of an horse!' Says Sylvia, in reply, —

'So far as to be troubled with neither spleen, cholic, nor vapours; I need no salts for my stomach, no hartshorn for my head, nor wash for my complexion. I can gallop all the morning after the hunting-horn, and all the evening after a fiddle. In short, I can do everything with my father but drink and shoot flying; and I 'm sure I could do everything my mother could, were I put to the trial.'

Then Melinda informs her that her captain has come to town.

'Ah, Melinda,' says she, 'now that he is

come, I 'll take care he sha' n't go without a companion.'

'You are certainly mad, cousin,' replies the other.

'And there 's a pleasure sure in being mad, which none but madmen know,' quotes she.

Then says Melinda, 'Thou poor romantic Quixote, hast thou the vanity to imagine that a young sprightly officer, that rambles o'er half the globe in half a year, can confine his thoughts to the little daughter of a country justice in an obscure part of the world?'

'Psha!' replies Sylvia, 'what care I for his thoughts? I should not like a man with confined thoughts; it shows a narrowness of soul. Constancy is but a dull, sleepy quality at best; they will hardly admit it among the manly virtues, nor do I think it deserves a place with bravery, knowledge, policy, justice, and some other qualities that are proper to that noble sex. In short, Melinda, I think a petticoat a mighty simple thing, and I am heartily tired of my sex.'

She is, of course, in love with Captain Plume, a gentleman of parts, who describes himself as having been 'constant to fifteen at a time, but never melancholy for one.' As by the death of her brother she comes in for fifteen hundred a

year, old Justice Ballance does not approve of
Captain Plume as an heir to his estate and
family, tells her she must think no more of him,
and bids her take coach and go into the country. This command she promises to obey ; but
in the third act she turns up in the apparel of
a beau, and enters on the scene whilst Plume
and Brazen — a very Cæsar among women,
and a recruiting officer likewise — are holding
conversation.

' Save ye, save ye, gentlemen ! ' says she.

' My dear, I 'm yours,' says Brazen, an impu-
dent fellow, in truth.

' Do you know the gentleman ? ' asks Plume.

' No, but I will presently,' says the other ;
and then he turns to the pretty young gentleman. ' Your name, my dear ? ' says he.

' Wilful,' says Sylvia, quite cute, — ' Jack Wilful, at your service.'

' What, the Kentish Wilfuls, or those of Staffordshire ? ' asks Captain Brazen.

' Both, sir, both ; I 'm related to all the Wilfuls in Europe, and I 'm the head of the family
at present.'

' Do you live in the country, sir ? ' asks
Plume, who, of course, does not recognise her
in this disguise which she has assumed.

' Yes, sir,' says she. ' I live where I stand ;

I have neither house, home, nor habitation beyond this spot of ground.'

' What are you, sir ? ' queries Brazen.

' A rake,' says she, plainly enough.

' In the army, I presume ? ' says Plume.

' No, but I intend to 'list immediately. Look 'e, gentlemen, he that bids the fairest has me.'

Then they both bid for this recruit ; says Brazen, ' Sir, I 'll prefer you ; I 'll make you a corporal this minute.'

' Corporal ! ' says Plume, '' I'll make you my companion ; you shall eat with me.'

' You shall drink with me,' says Brazen.

' You shall lie with me, you young rogue,' says Plume.

' You shall receive your pay and do no duty,' says the other, bidding yet higher.

' Then,' says Sylvia, ' you must make me a field-officer.'

This latter little joke was one which the audience invariably received with great relish. Presently Sylvia, who does not just yet enlist with either of these gallant gentlemen, objects to Plume's too friendly advances towards a certain Rose, a young market-woman ; but the captain assures her on this delicate point, for, says he, philosophically enough, it must be

admitted, ' The women, you know, are the load-
stones everywhere ; gain the wives, and you are
caressed by the husbands ; please the mistress,
and you are valued by the gallants ; secure an
interest with the finest women at Court, and
you procure the favour of the greatest men ; so
kiss the prettiest wenches, and you are secure
of 'listing the lustiest fellows.'

Finally Sylvia is discovered by her wearing
a suit of clothes belonging to her late brother,
is forgiven by her father, married to the man
she loves, and all ends as happily as may be.

Now for weeks previous the town was anxious to see the Woffington in this favourite character, the representation of which required so
much spirit and vivacity ; and when, on the
night of her first appearance, she was, in the
second scene of the first act, discovered in an
apartment, her mere appearance won upon the
audience, and gained her a hearty round of applause. Slightly above the middle height, her
figure had a symmetry and flexibility which lent
a natural grace to her every movement ; whilst
her luminous eyes, beautiful complexion, slightly
aquiline nose, and tender lips, completed a picture that charmed even to fascination.   Then
the ease of her manner, the justness of her gestures, the rapt expression of her face that seemed

to reflect her speech, rendered her such an actress as had not been seen for years.   Her playing, indeed, was nature and not art.   To those
present it seemed that up to this hour wooden-
limbed, painted-faced puppets had strutted me-
chanically across the stage, uttering speeches
that lost their point, and became limp and dull
on falling from their lips ; but now, such is the
effect of genius, her mere presence amongst them
seemed to endow them with souls, and trans-
form them from marionettes to men and women
with hearts and human passions.

Presently, when this charming woman came
on the stage in the apparel of a pretty gentleman about town, with a red coat, a sword, a
hat *bien trouffée*, a martial twist in his cravat, a
fierce knot in his periwig, a cane hanging from
his button, the effect was marvellous.   Her air
was at once graceful and rakish ; her delivery
pert and pointed ; the witchery of her glances
was pronounced inimitable.   There were no
two opinions regarding her, pronounced in the
coffee-houses that night ; for all admitted that
the satisfaction she afforded was beyond expression.   By desire ' The Recruiting Officer '
was repeated for three nights running, — a by
no means inconsiderable compliment to the actress's powers in those days, when a fresh play

was as a rule performed nightly. Her praise
quickly reached the Court, and the Duke of
Cumberland, and the Princesses Amelia, Caroline, and Louisa bespoke a play in which she
was to appear ; to wit, ' The Double Gallant,'
or the ' Sick Lady's Cure.' This was the occasion of her eighth appearance, and she was
much applauded in the character she represented, that of Lady Sadlife. Subsequently she
played Aura in ' The Country Lasses ; ' and on
the 21st of November she appeared, ' by particular desire,' for the first time in London, as
Sir Harry Wildair in the comedy of ' The Constant Couple, or a Trip to the Jubilee,' by
Farquhar.

Sir Harry Wildair was a character scarce
second in favour to Sylvia with the town ; both
having that dash and brilliancy which suited
the complexion of the times. Sir Harry was a
spark just come from France, and was at once
the joy of the playhouses and the life of the
park. He was brave and gay ; a gentleman of
happy circumstances ; a plentiful estate, and a
genteel education, which left him as free from
rigidness in his morals as his constitution rendered him liberal in his pleasures. His humorous gaiety and the freedom of his behaviour —
airy after the fashion of the times, yet tempered

ROBERT WILKS Esq.

with honour — are skilfully pourtrayed in the series of his love adventures which constitute the comedy. This part had been first played by Wilks, who had some claims to be considered a man of quality, and who made the representation of men about town his special study. So clever was his personation of Sir Harry, that it set him above the competition of all other actors of his time, and gained him that praise due to his great merit. Farquhar said that when the stage had the misfortune to lose him, Sir Harry might go to the —— Jubilee. And since Wilks had taken his exit from this world's stage (now almost ten years ago) no other had been found to play the part with justness and spirit.

The attempt of this new actress was therefore looked for with eager curiosity by the public, and with some apprehension by her friends : feelings that, on her appearance, were changed to admiration and delight. In the well-bred rake of quality, who lightly tripped across the stage, singing a blithe song, and followed by two footmen, there was no trace of the woman. The audience beheld only a young man of faultless figure, distinguished by an ease of manner, polish of address, and nonchalance that at once surprised and fascinated them. Seldom had a player in one night attained such success. ' So

infinitely did she surpass expectation,' says Tate
Wilkinson, in his memoirs, ' that the applause
she received was beyond any at that time ever
known. An elegant figure, she looked and
acted Sir Harry Wildair with such spirit and
deportment, that she gave flat contradiction to
what Farquhar asserted,— that when Wilks died
Sir Harry might go to the —— Jubilee.' Her
success became the conversation of every polite circle, as well as in every tavern and coffee-
house in town, from St. Paul's to St. James's ;
and so crowded were the houses it drew, that
the part was repeated for twenty consecutive
nights,—a fact significantly marking her triumph
and establishing her favour.

She subsequently played during the season
Elvira, in the ' Spanish Fryar ; ' Violante, in the
' Double Falsehood ; ' Laetitia, in Congreve's
' Old Bachelor ; ' Amanda, in Cibber's ' Love's
Last Shift ; ' and Phillis, in Steele's ' Conscious
Lovers.' In all of these she was successful ;
for, aware that the public was a patron worth
pleasing, she took infinite pains in all that concerned her profession ; made up with great care
and judgment suitable to the part ; committed
her lines to mind (a practice that did not always
obtain in her day), and strove to realize the
author's ideal in the characters she assumed.

Her reward came quickly in the appreciation freely awarded her. She was installed as a favourite in the public mind, — a position she retained during her bright, brief career. Praise of her rare beauty — a vast help to such talents as hers — was likewise on every tongue ; the poets penned sonnets to her ; the print-sellers sold her ·portraits ; and as Conway wrote to Walpole of her, in this her first season, ' All the town is in love with her.'

CHAPTER V.

Peg Woffington's Engagement at Drury Lane. — Kitty Clive, her Passion for Tragedy. — Delane the Student of T. C. D. — Macklin and his Adventures. — The Turning-point of his Career. — His Wonderful Shylock. — What Mr. Pope said. — Young David Garrick. — His Early Life at Lichfield. — Becomes a Wine-merchant. — Among the Critics at the Bedford. — Hesitates to go on the Stage. — Falls in Love with Peg Woffington. — In the Green-room at Drury Lane. — Sir Charles Hanbury Williams. — The Woffington's Definition of an Age.

TOWARDS the end of the season — in May, 1741 — Peg Woffington ceased to act in the Covent Garden playhouse, owing to a disagreement with Rich ; and on the 19th of the month the following quaint advertisement appeared in the ' London Daily Post ' : —

' Covent Garden. — Whereas, some persons principally concerned in the Play of the Rehearsal, etc., being indisposed, is the reason the same cannot be performed as Advertised in Saturday and Yesterday's Bills ; on this account the Company are obliged to take this Method of returning Thanks to the Town for all their Favours, and humbly take their Leave till next Season.'

MRS. BENNET.

Four months later, at the commencement of the winter season, she appeared as Sylvia on the boards of Drury Lane Theatre, of which Fleetwood was then manager. Mrs. Pritchard, an excellent actress, who had the previous season played the leading parts at Drury Lane, now went over to Covent Garden, where she ventured to play the part of Sylvia ; but as her strength lay in the representation of tragic heroines, she did not win the applause which invariably attended the Woffington's personation of that favourite character.

At Drury Lane there was a strong company this season, which numbered amongst its ladies Kitty Clive, Mrs. Butler, and Mrs. Bennet, whilst the male element was represented by Theo Cibber, Macklin, Delane, Milward, and Raftor. Quin was at this time playing in Dublin and the Irish provinces.

Kitty Clive, plain of face, warm of temper, sharp of tongue, was pleased to regard the Woffington as her rival. Kitty had made her *début* as a page in ' Mithridates King of Pontus ' in the Drury Lane playhouse, about the same time as Peg Woffington made her first bow to the audience assembled in Madame Violante's booth ; but Kitty was then in her seventeenth year, whilst Peggy had but reached her tenth.

This page which the youthful Kitty represented was not quite a mute creature, with no better task than supporting a train or carrying a cup, but had a song to sing proper to the circumstances of the scene, which was received with extraordinary applause. But from pages in silken hose, velvet jerkin, and feathered cap, she grad- ·ually worked her way to better parts. She had once by her singing forced a reluctant audience · to give a hearing to Colley Cibber's ' Love in a Riddle,' — a favour denied to His Gracious Majesty of the following night ; she had likewise been called ' a charming little devil ' by one of the pretty fellows in the stage box ; and presently she laid claims to be considered a great comic actress by her bright, blithesome rendering of Nell in ' The Devil to Pay,' a ballad farce of Coffey's, as well as by her representation of singing chambermaids (chambermaids always sang in those days), hoydens, romps, and vulgar fine ladies.

But she who had been styled ' a charming little devil ' possessed a soul that loftily soared above comedy to the sublime regions of tragedy; and her greatest delight in life was to play such parts as Ophelia, Desdemona, and Portia. Under her treatment these characters were little less than burlesques ; especially when, in the

trial scene, she as Portia introduced comic business, and mimicked to the life the famous Lord
Mansfield, whose peculiarities were the laughing-stock of the town. Kitty was altogether a
person of vast importance ; she was the daughter of an Irish gentleman,—one William Raftor,
a native of the city of Kilkenny, who had been
bred to the law, and whose property had been
forfeited to the Crown by reason of his having
followed the fortunes of James the Second and
fought on the side of that unhappy monarch at
the famous Battle of the Boyne. Moreover,
she had married a brother of Baron Clive, and
was the friend of Horace Walpole, who was in
himself a gentleman of the highest quality, and
a patron of all the arts. Though she parted
from her husband soon after her marriage, no
breath of scandal then, or throughout her career,
was ever attached to her name. According to
Arthur Murphy, she was 'a diamond of the first
water,' but like a diamond she could cut deeply,
for her tongue was as steel ; and frequently she
would aim one of her bitter speeches at this new
actress, who had in one night gained the fame
which it had taken her, the Clive, years to establish, — which speeches the Woffington would
return in kind, but with a charming coolness
that sent her hot-tempered rival furious. In all

her battles Kitty was loyally supported by her
brother Jemmy Raftor, a very indifferent actor,
but a genuine Irishman, who had the characteristic talent of telling a humourous story and turning a pretty compliment with wonderful ease.

But in the ranks of the Drury Lane company
the Woffington had a more friendly face turned
towards her in that of young Delane, the son
of an Irish gentleman, who had been a student
at Trinity College when she had sold oranges
and water-cresses to the ' college boys,' and entertained them with her wit.   His friends had
destined him for the Church ; but the stage had
more attractions for him than the pulpit, and to
their infinite disgust he became a player.   In
the same year that the Woffington appeared as
the pupil of Madame Violante, he was engaged
at the Aungier Street Theatre by Elrington.
Singularly handsome, with a graceful figure
and a full-toned voice, he had the principal ac-
quirements which constitute a good actor.   For
three years he played in Dublin ; at the end of
which time he, like most of his countrymen
then and now, was tempted by the more liberal
rewards held out to talent by the sister country, and came to London.   His first engagement was at the Goodman's Fields Theatre ; but
he subsequently enlisted under Fleetwood's

SOUTHWARK FAIR.

management, and played the romantic heroes
at Drury Lane.

Charles Macklin, another member of the company, was also a countryman of the Woffington's, and soon became her friend. A lineal
descendant of an Irish king, a runaway 'prentice of an Irish saddler, he had been in his day
a strolling player ; had acted Hamlet and harlequin the same night ; had passed as a vagrant
and a vagabond, played in barns, had starved,
been houseless, and had strutted his brief hour
in a booth at Southwark Fair. He had been
known in his earlier days as 'the wild Irishman,'
and had been called ' Wicked Charley.' Being
a Bohemian by nature and profession, his adventures were many, curious, and amusing ; and
when he became garrulous in his old age, the
narration of these used to afford him and his
friends much diversion. Amongst other stories,
he used to tell that he and merry Dick Ashby,
a dissipated fellow enough, the son of a Dublin
manager, went into a gambling-house by way of
having a frolic one night, when he, Macklin,
won over a hundred guineas, a sum that seemed
to him inexhaustible. Accordingly next day he
and his friend, attended by two ladies of the
town, went down to St. Albans, to take the air,
and enjoy the pleasures of the country. One

night this gay little party went to a public ball.
and being very expensively dressed, they passed
as people of condition, until one of the ladies,
getting into a dispute concerning the priority of
place in a country dance, her language and
temper discovered her profession ; when she
and her companion were handed out of the
room, and the gentlemen received a hint that
it was desirable for them to follow.

But at this time, when Woffington joined the
Drury Lane company, Macklin was in the
meridian of life. He had sown his wild oats,
had married and settled down, and had proved
himself a very useful actor. He had played
such characters as Touchstone in 'As You Like
It,' and Sir Francis Wronghead in 'The Provoked Husband,' with great success ; but he
had at heart a great desire to play another character more important than these. So one day
he summoned courage to petition Fleetwood,
the manager, to allow him to act Shylock in
'The Merchant of Venice' for just one night.
He had long studied the character, and on his
representation of the Jew he was satisfied to
let his reputation rest for ever. After some
persuasion the manager consented, to Macklin's vast delight ; and 'The Merchant of Venice,' 'written by Shakespeare,' was speedily

announced for performance. In order to render the play more palatable to the public, it was set forth that the part of Lorenzo would be played by Mr. Lowe, 'in which will be introduced songs proper to the play, with entertainments of dancing by Signor and Signora Fansau, viz., Le Genereux Corsair, with cloaths and decorations entirely new.' The bills furthermore added that, 'as no money will be taken for the future behind the scenes, 't is hop'd that none will take it ill they can't be admitted there.'

Now, heretofore the character of the Jew had been played as a low-comedy part by all actors ; nay, even the celebrated Doggett had played it in the style of a broad farce. But Macklin was resolved to depart from old traditions, and for one night at least to present the Jew as a serious character. Rumour of this resolution having got abroad, the company generally regarded it as a joke ; but finding that Macklin was serious in his determination, they requested the manager to make him give up a part, his playing of which would bring disgrace on them all. Fleetwood fled in consternation to Macklin, who merely said he would pledge his life on the success of the play. What his intended treatment of the Jew really was, none

could tell ; for at the rehearsal he merely spoke
his lines in an undertone, unaccompanied by
gestures.   But those who were to play with
him entertained many fears concerning his representation, — especially when it was remembered that Rich had once dismissed him for
not declaiming in the stilted orthodox manner
when he played a tragedy part, and had treated
it ' too familiarly,' to use the phrase of the
harlequin manager.   If he had then departed
from the beaten track, what might he not do
now with the comical Jew ?   There was no
knowing.

At last the eventful night arrived on which
Macklin was satisfied to rest his future theatrical reputation.   Kitty Clive was cast for her
favourite part as Portia, the Woffington as
Nerissa, and Delane for the Merchant.   When
Macklin made his appearance in the green-
room, dressed for the part, he wore a piqued
beard, a loose black gown tied with a coloured
sash, and a red hat ; for, as he subsequently
explained to Pope, he had read that Jews
in Italy, especially in Venice, wore hats of
that colour.   Moreover, his face was carefully
painted, and the lines on his brow and cheeks
well marked.   Those in the green-room stared
at him with wonder.   There was no trace of the

comic element in this Hebrew. Their worst
fears were now confirmed.

' Look at his face ! ' whispered one of them.

'Why,' says another, 'if Almighty God writes
a legible hand, Macklin must be a villain.'

Then out spoke Kitty Clive, who was already
dressed as Portia, and expected to create great
mirth in that part. 'Sure,' says she, ' no one
ever saw such a Jew.'

' Did you expect to see him wear a couple
of hats, and carry a bag on his back, ma'am ? '
asks the Woffington, with an air of innocent
curiosity.

' No, Peggy, no more than I expected to
see him carry an orange-basket on his arm,'
replies the smart-tongued lady, turning quickly
away.

Meanwhile, Macklin nervously paced the room,
muttering his lines in an undertone, until Delane, coming in, announced that the house was
crowded from top to bottom ; whereon the Jew
went on the stage, and looking through a slit
in the curtain, saw the news was true, and felt
gratified. The two front rows of the pit were
already crowded with critics, wearing the air
of men who had come to pass a highly diverting
evening. ' Ahem ! ' said Macklin, with his eye
at the slit ; ' I shall be tried to-night by a

special jury.' His heart sank ; was he wise,
after all, in his determination of playing the
Jew as a serious character ? His whole future
as a player depended on this night. As he
turned away in nervous impatience, he felt a
hand placed gently on his arm, and looking up,
encountered two luminous eyes that shone upon
him comfortingly in the semi-gloom of the great
stage, and heard Peg Woffington's voice whisper, ' Courage, Mac, courage ! Show them
you can act.' In another second the stage was
cleared, and the bell for the curtain rang with a
merry little peal that seemed to him to carry
rejoicement and assurance with it ; and moreover, the tone was like to the voice that had
just spoken words of hope in his ear.

The heavy green curtain went up with many
a creak ; the actors commenced their parts.
Macklin's heart began to flutter wildly ; ' but
commending my cause to Providence,' says he,
' I went boldly on the stage.' He was received with some applause, though his appearance caused general surprise. Then came the
terrible hour of judgment, in which he was to
be set down as one who had read Shakespeare
aright, or as a fool who had dared to ignore the
traditions handed down to him by his betters.
The opening scenes were tame and level ; but

from those terrible front rows in the pit, which
had seemed at first bristling with sarcasm and
mocking hilarity, he caught the words, ' Very
well, — very well indeed ; this man seems to
know what he is about.' Which praise, though
faint, had the grateful effect of warming him to
his work. A night, a week, ay, whole years
seemed to have passed over his head before the
third act came, for which he had reserved all
his strength in contrasting the passions of joy
and triumph for the merchant's losses with grief
and despair for Jessica's elopement. In be-
wailing her loss he rushed upon the stage
hatless, his face distorted by rage, his eyes
bewildered, his hands fiercely clutched, his
every movement abrupt and convulsive. Never
had his audience seen such a representation of
the Jew ; but though new to them, they felt an
echo in their hearts which told them it was true
to nature. Then came the most vehement applause ; the whole house was in an uproar ; he
was saved, his success was assured. At the
trial scene all elements of burlesque were abolished ; even Kitty Clive did not for once venture on her mimicry of Lord Mansfield. In
this culminating scene a veritable Shylock stood
upon the stage, — merciless, full of the passions
of hatred and revenge ; and so intensely were

they pourtrayed, that when he whetted the glit-
tering knife which was to cut away the pound
of flesh, the whole house shuddered. Never
had there been such acting, and seldom such
applause as rang through the house when the
curtain descended.

The green-room presented a curious appearance at the conclusion of the performance.
Here were assembled the nobility and critics, -
— some of the former adorned with stars and
garters, and all of them clad in velvets of many
colours and satins of rich sheen ; and mixing
amongst them, in the freest manner possible,
were the actors and actresses, scarcely less brilliant in the richness of their sixteenth-century
Venetian costumes. What bows were changed,
what compliments were paid, what judgments
were passed ! Every one was now elated by
the triumph, as if it had been a personal matter ; and when Macklin came into the room, a
crowd pressed round him ready to offer him a
thousand congratulations.

‘ Ah, Macklin, you were right, after all ! ’
said Fleetwood, shaking him heartily by the
hand.

‘ And may I ask, Mrs. Clive,’ says Fielding,
going over to that lady, who was yet attired in
the gown of one pertaining to the law, ‘ why

you did not give us your imitation of the great man to-night ? '

' In faith,' says honest Kitty Clive, ' when I looked at Shylock, I was afraid.'

Then up went Peg Woffington to the hero of the hour. ' An' sure,' says she in an aside, assuming a broad brogue as she spoke, ' it takes an Irishman to tache them what a Jew is like.'

' God bless you, Peggy ! ' said he, in the same tone, and his voice trembled a little. ' Your words made a man of me.'

' Arrah, whist, Charley Macklin ! sure, it 's yourself always had the palavering tongue,' answered she, archly ; and then she slipped away, for others pressed forward to greet him.

Presently there was a stir and bustle in the far end of the green-room, and a group of be-wigged and beruffled gentlemen came slowly along, bowing their heads, and occasionally laughing mighty heartily, in answer to the remarks of a thin-legged little gentleman, de-murely dressed in black, who walked in the centre of this human cluster. This little gen-tleman in black had a remarkable-looking coun-tenance, with dark-looking eyes, and eyebrows that seemed to occupy undue space in the up-per part of his face. When he came to where

Macklin stood, he paused, as did those surrounding him likewise ; a faded smile crossed
his thin lips, and rippling upwards, caught the
sparkle of his eyes before it lost itself in the
wrinkles of his forehead. Then he helped himself leisurely to snuff, resting both his bony
hands on his gold-knobbed cane, and looked
the actor full in the face. Macklin trembled
as he glanced down at him, for he knew well
that a biting epigram or a sarcastic phrase uttered by these thin lips would be repeated in
every coffee-house and tavern in town on the
morrow.

‘ May I venture to hope,’ he said, speaking
with a big voice to hide his nervousness, and
bowing with quaint theatric grace, ‘ that my
poor efforts to-night have given the great Mr.
Pope some slight satisfaction ? ’

The little gentleman smiled again ; those
around him bent their heads in one common
movement, to catch his words ; then, pointing
his forefinger to Macklin, he said, —

> ‘ This is the Jew
> That Shakespeare drew.’

Poor Macklin, overwhelmed by the compliment, bowed half way to the ground ; the group
surrounding the little gentleman cried, ‘ Excellent ! — prodigiously fine ! ’ and without another

POPE.

word he went out of the green-room, surrounded
by his courtiers, to where his coach waited him
in the lane. The couplet, which has outlived
the poet who uttered it, and the actor to whom
it was applied, was repeated all over the town
that night. ' Gad, sìr,' Macklin would say long
years after, when recounting the glories of this
memorable evening over a bottle of old port in
a snug box at the Bedford, — ' gad, sir, though
I was not worth fifty pounds in the world at that
time, let me tell you I was Charles the Great
for that night.'

During the Woffington's first season at Drury
Lane there frequently came to the green-room
of the theatre ' a very sprightly young man,
neatly made ; ' whose bright face, singularly mobile, and remarkable, moreover, for its luminous
eyes, at once attracted the actress's attention.
This was David Garrick, a character destined
to play an important part in the drama of Peg
Woffington's life. His father, a gentleman of
French origin, had been an officer in the English army, whose regiment was for several years
stationed at Lichfield. Here the captain married
a lady descended on the maternal side from an
Irish family, who bore him ten children. The
third of these was David, who grew into a lad
full of brightness and promise, showing amongst

his other talents a turn for mimicry and recitation. He had, indeed, at the age of ten, indicated where the bent of his genius lay, by
forming a few of his schoolfellows and his sisters
into a theatrical company, which, under his
direction, performed Farquhar's ' Recruiting
Officer ' before a considerable audience.   A
year later and the sprightly lad was sent to
Portugal to his uncle, a prosperous wine-merchant, who had promised to establish him in his
house.   But the wine trade had no attraction
for David, and in little more than twelve months
he returned to Lichfield once more, to a home
that would have been happy but for its stings of
petty poverty.   To strive and remedy this lack
of fortune, Captain Garrick went to Gibraltar
two years after his son's return from Portugal ;
the exile from his affectionate but large family
being in some measure compensated for by a
pay double the amount of that he had previously
enjoyed.   But even with that portion of it which
he allowed his delicate and desponding wife and
seven surviving children, life was to them a long-
continued struggle to sustain a shabby gentility
in the eyes of their Lichfield neighbours.

During the captain's residence in what was
known as ' foreign parts,' David, then a lad of
fourteen, seems to have been the member of the

family who was selected to carry on a correspondence with the absent head of his house.
These letters, presented to the Dyce and Forster
Library in the South Kensington Museum, by
the late John Forster, are marvellously interesting. Some of them tell stories of a poverty
which, though occasionally galling, never called
forth a complaint, but was ever borne with a
brave show of cheerfulness.

'My mamma received the £30 you was so
good as to send,' says David, in the earliest
of these clearly written epistles, commencing
with 'Hon. Sir,' and directed in big schoolboy
characters 'To Captain Garrick, on Brigadier
Kirk's Regiment at Gibraltar.' 'She paid £10
to Mr. Rider, one year's rent; and £10 to ye
baker, and if you can spare a little more, or tell
her you will, she is in hopes of paying all ye
debt, that you may have nothing to fret you
when you come home.' The Captain took the
hint as to sparing a little more, for presently
David writes, 'My mamma sends her dearest
Love and affection to you, and desires me to
tell you she has cleared almost the Debts, except a little to ye Butcher, which she hopes to
clear in a month or two.' Then the poor Captain in foreign parts has to learn that they are
so 'very shabby in cloathes and in all our ac-

coutrements, that we was rather like so many
beggars than Gentlemen Soldiers.' The poor
wife at home ' has been nursing one of her
daughters, who lay ill, amost six months, and
has become unwell herself and is ordered to
drink wine, which is sorely against her inclination, as her pocket cannot afford it.' Then
' my sister Lenny and sister Jenny,' writes
young Davy to his father, ' send their Duty to
you, and being in great want for some Lace for
their Heads, and my Mamma being but very
low in ye Purse, by reason of her illness, could
not afford y^m so much money, they with ye
greatest Duty and Obedience request a small
matter to purchase their Head Ornaments.
Great necessity compels them to give you this
trouble, for they have never worn anything else
but plain Head Cloathes, which hardly distinguishes them from ye vulgar madams.'

The lad has had a present made him by Mr.
Hervey, lately come from London, of ' two pair
of large silver buckles, one pair for my shoes,
and ye other for ye Breeches knees.' But alas !
what use are the latter, if young David has no
decent breeches to wear. Perhaps his father
will take the hint ; but alas ! the Captain in foreign parts has a mind that does not readily receive suggestions where money is concerned,

and his son after waiting a long time is obliged
to speak plainly.

'I must tell my dear papa,' writes he, approaching the subject in a wily manner, 'that I
am quite turned Philosopher; you perhaps may
think me vain, but to show you I am not, I
would gladly get shut of my characteristick of
a philosopher, viz. a ragged pair of breeches.
Now, the only way you have to cure your son
of his philosophick qualification is to send some
handsome thing for a waistcoat, and pair of
breeches to hide his nakedness. They tell me
velvet is very cheap at Gibraltar. Amen, and so
be it!' No wonder he · began the world,' as
Johnson said, ' with a great hunger for money,'
for, as the philosopher used to remark, ' he was
bred in a family whose study was to make fourpence do as much as others made fourpence
halfpenny do.'

The poor wife, who had borne him ten children, and whose health was now shattered,
writes to her absent husband occasionally, not
of the poverty of her home, but, like a true
wife, of the riches of that love which lay stored
for him in her faithful heart. ' Dear life and
soul,' she calls him tenderly ; and then comes
a confession that must have been sweet indeed
to the exile. ' I am not able,' she says, ' to

live easy longer without you ; for I grow very
jealous. But in the midst of all this, I do not
blame my dear. I have very sad dreams for
you, but I have the pleasure when I am up to
think, were I with you, how tender my dear
soul would be to me ; nay, was, when I was
with you last. Oh that I had you in my arms!
I would tell my dear life how much I am his.'
Then David testifies in a charming manner to
the affection of his mother for his father. Speaking of a miniature of the Captain's which the lad
says he would sooner have one glance at than
look a whole day at the finest picture in the
world, he tells his father, ' My poor mamma
sighs whenever she passes the picture.' And
again he adds, ' My mamma sends her most
tender affections. She says your presence would
do her more good than all the physicians in Europe.' She has ' a fever upon her spirits,' and
is sadly depressed by the absence of him whom
she loves, and whom she thinks of by day and
dreams of by night ; and when he has been
away for some two years, she can bear the separation no longer, and has a scheme for bringing
him back to England which young Davy re-
veals to his father.

　' My mamma,' says he, ' designs to try her
interest to get you leave to come over by next

spring, if you are not sent for over before. She designs to apply first to the Brigadeer. My mamma will get Mr. Hervey to write her a pretty Letter to ye Brigadeer ye Purpot of it shall be this, that you having a son to put out, and my mamma being uncapable to do it herself, it would be a great detriment to the Family if you was not here to do it yourself; and as soon as Mr. Hervey has done it, my mamma will copy it, and sent it to Mr. Adair to give it to ye Brigadeer.'

After an absence of about three years, Captain Garrick returned, and David was sent to a school advertised in the ' Gentleman's Magazine ' as ' at Edial, near Lichfield, in Staffordshire, where young gentlemen are taught the Latin and Greek Languages by Samuel Johnson.' The said Samuel Johnson, whose father was a bookseller in Lichfield, was well known to David Garrick, who, in common with his fellow scholars, had but little reverence for their master's learning. They laughed at his uncouth gesticulations and the oddities of his manner; whilst Mrs. Johnson, a lady described by Garrick to Boswell as ' very fat, with a bosom of more than ordinary protuberance, with swelled cheeks, of a florid red, produced by thick painting, and increased by the liberal use of cordials ; flaring and fantastic in her dress, and affected both in her speech and her general behaviour,' was a fruitful source for David's mimicry. 'The young rogues,' says Boswell, speaking of this time, ' used to listen at the door of his bedchamber, and peep through the keyhole, that they might turn into ridicule his tumultuous and awkward fondness for Mrs. Johnson, whom he used to name by the familiar appellation of Tetty or Tetsey, which, like Betty or Betsey, is provincially used as a contraction for Elizabeth, her Christian name, but which seems ludicrous when applied to a woman of her age and appearance.'

Johnson's Academy had a short life, if a merry one, and when its doors closed Garrick and he went up to town; Johnson having a tragedy, and twopence halfpenny in his pocket, as he used to recount in his palmier days, with a humorous twinkle in his eyes. Garrick entered himself as a student of the Honourable Society of Lincoln's Inn, paying as fees, ' for the use of this society, the sum of three pounds, three shillings, and fourpence.' Then he went to study under Mr. Colson, ' a rational philosopher,' the chief purpose for which he had left his home. This was an eventful year in his life. Scarce a month had elapsed from the day on which he had departed from Lichfield

LINCOLN'S INN.

when news came to him of his father's death ;
his mother quickly followed to the grave the
man she had loved all her life ; and finally came
the demise of the Lisbon wine-merchant, who
left his nephew and namesake a legacy of one
thousand pounds sterling.

All idea of studying for the law was now abandoned, and it was decided that David Garrick
and his brother Peter, his senior by six years,
should set up as partners in the wine trade, —
Peter to conduct the business in Lichfield, and
David in Durham Yard, situated at the end
of one of the smaller streets leading from the
Strand. Here, as Foote afterwards said, he
lived, ' with three quarts of vinegar in a cellar,
and called himself a wine-merchant.' David
soon showed he had no talent for business, and
paid it but little heed ; to the great disgust of
his elder brother, a man of very different cast,
—formal, methodical, and industrious, who even
at this time entertained a wholesome horror of
his brother's predilection for the company of
players. But fate, it seemed, favoured David's
passion for the society of those connected in any
way with the playhouses, inasmuch as Durham
Yard was within a stone's throw of Covent
Garden, and that the space which lay between
swarmed with the coffee-houses, taverns, and

ordinaries where the sons of Thespis most did
congregate. With all of them Garrick made
friends ; his bright face, ready ways, and pleasant manners being certain passports to the good
fellowship of a race then and now proverbially
genial.

At those ordinaries or coffee-houses he spent
that portion of the day which was not devoted
to the study of Shakespeare at his desk. Then
at night he would sit in the pit of Drury Lane
or Covent Garden, watching Delane's graceful
lovers or Theo Cibber's fops ; after which he
would hie him to the Bedford, the recognized
emporium of wit and criticism, where he would
listen to plain-faced Jemmy Raftor tell one of
his droll Irish stories, or hear Ryan discourse
in his discontented, piping voice, of the traditional glory of all things dramatic in the past,
and of their worthlessness in the present.

' You should have seen the great Wilks, sir,'
he would say ; ' ah ! he was an actor, and his
were the days when good acting might be seen
at the playhouse ' (here a pinch of snuff) ; ' and
Betterton, sir, whose awe-inspiring Hamlet can
never again be equalled ; and then Barton Booth,
a gentleman, sir, and a player of prodigious
merit.' But 't was sure the old school was
dead ; the old traditions had passed away for-

ever (here a grave shake of his head). Perhaps some trace lingered yet in his own playing; it was not for him to say, but he had received great commendations for his Richard the Third, that was true ; and he had the honour of being instructed in the part of Marcus in the tragedy of ' Cato ' by its author, the great Mr. Addison himself. Then followed a chorus of critics who had sat in the front rows of the pit, and spoke learnedly of the play, praised the stormy mouthing of Bridgewater or Walker, the stiff-jointed love-making of Milward, or damned some trembling aspirant to fame, as lightly as they took a pinch of snuff. Now and then Garrick would add his voice, and lay down his opinions with all the self-assertion of youth. Amongst the company with which he freely mixed, he singled out two men as his especial friends ; these were Macklin of Drury Lane, and Giffard, the manager of the Goodman's Fields playhouse. With these kindred spirits he frequently lamented the condition to which the stage was reduced, where nature was wholly ignored, and false principles of art supplied in its place. Comedy was boldly reduced to farce that frequently bordered on buffoonery, passion was interpreted by inflated ranting, love made its protestations in a measured drawl, whilst the ordinary dialogue was

delivered in a set, monotonous tone, most weari-
some to the ear.   Macklin would call to mind
his dismissal for speaking a part too familiarly,
and his recent success in playing Shylock with
realism ; and Giffard was of opinion that the
town submitted to the present school of acting
merely for want of knowing better.   Then the
young wine-merchant would show them how
comedy should be played according to his thinking, — how the jest should flow from the lips
naturally and promptly, the laugh come freely
as if honestly enjoyed, the facial expression
suiting the words and action.   Then, as to
tragedy, he would show them how he would
play Hamlet if he were an actor.   The young
Dane on beholding his father's ghost should be
fixed in mute astonishment, his cheeks should
gradually grow pale, his eyes blaze from fear
and horror, his voice tremble, as he questioned
the visitor from an unknown sphere.   Then in
the scene with Ophelia, he should feign madness by look and gesture, and the expression of
his speech ; and to the Queen he should speak
daggers to rend her heart with sorrow and re-
morse ; and as Garrick illustrated his conceptions by gesture, tone, and facial expression,
the two actors, standing mutely by, would look
at and listen to him with surprise, glancing at

each other significantly and nodding their heads
sagely. Then they would both urge him to
give up trade and take to the stage, for they
were sure he had the makings of a great actor
in him.

But this was a suggestion which, though his
heart bounded forward to follow it, he was
loath to put into practice. All the traditional
prejudices of caste handed down to him by the
struggling captain in a walking regiment and
his genteel wife with relatives in the Church,
and carefully maintained by the highly respectable wine-merchant in Lichfield and his sisters,
rose in David's mind, and for a time held him
back from the calling of a player. An actor
was indeed in those days considered a veritable
vagabond, — a worthless, godless creature, the
fitting object for the censure and disdain of his
fellow-creature. More than twenty years later,
when Garrick's example might be supposed to
have in some measure mitigated such opinions,
Horace Walpole, the elegant patron of arts,
lamenting in the bitterness of his heart Lady
Susan Strangeways' marriage with ' O'Brien the
actor,' — a man of irreproachable character, the
descendant of an old Irish family ruined by its
adherence to James II., — declares this union
' the completion of disgrace. Even a footman

were preferable. The publicity of the hero's profession,' adds this fine gentleman, the descendant of an honest timber merchant, ' perpetuates the mortification. I could not have believed that Lady Susan would have stooped so low.'

To become a player was therefore not a step for Garrick to take without consideration and apprehension. Meanwhile, as may well be supposed, the wine trade did not prosper; and when sober Peter Garrick came up to town, he found his partner and brother restless and unhappy. ' All my Illness and lowness of Spirits,' he subsequently wrote to Peter, when he had made the great plunge, ' was owing to my want of resolution to tell you my thoughts when here.' But before he had taken the decisive step, and whilst he was yet struggling with his inclinations, he had made the acquaintance of the Irish actress who had taken the town by storm. Night after night young Garrick was found amongst the crowds which flocked to see her at Covent Garden and Drury Lane, nor had she a more enthusiastic admirer than he. Here was an actress after his own heart, — one who neither reduced comedy to burlesque, nor tragedy to rant, but who was at one with Nature. He noted that her style had the effect of electrifying

HORACE WALPOLE.

her audiences ; and this gave him strong hopes
of at least finding a patient hearing, if ever, indeed, he came to seek his fortune on the boards.
It was only natural that this bright-looking young
man, full of enthusiasm for the stage, should tell
this charming creature with the soft eyes, tender
lips, and graceful ways, all that he thought of
her as an actress, and much that he felt for her
as a woman ; and Peggy, with her susceptible
Hibernian heart, listened to his earnest voice,
looked into his flashing eyes, and loved him.
And oh, what a happy time this was for both of
them, with all life before them ; with such
golden dreams of fame in their heads ; with such
warm love in their hearts ! In the spacious,
high-ceilinged green-room of old Drury Lane,
with its great oak fire-place, curiously carved,
and running half-way up the wall ; its ponderous-
framed pictures of Nell Gwyn and Congreve ;
its dust-covered bust of Shakespeare ; its great
settle, capable of accommodating a dozen persons, drawn close up by the fire ; its faded
crimson-velvet curtains pulled across the high,
narrow windows, Garrick would wait in the
evenings, with ever a laugh and jest on his lips
for the group around him, but with his eye
turned anxiously to the door as if he expected
some one to enter every minute. Presently

the door would be flung wide open, and the
imperious, graceful figure of Peg Woffington
would sweep in, dressed as Sylvia or as Lady
Betty Modish. Then her lover would join her,
and they would sit in some quiet corner of the
big room, dimly lighted by a sconce of wax
tapers above the chimney-piece, his hand touching hers, her eyes flashing on him in the full
radiance of her love, whilst they whispered each
other volumes of the airiest nothings in the
world ; disagreeing to agree, and painting ver-
bal portraits of each other that borrowed won-
drous colours from the light of their mutual
passion.

Then he would take from his pocket a copy
of the ' Gentleman's Magazine ' just published,
and read for her some verses, with which he
seemed most familiar, and which were addressed
to Sylvia, and signed ' G.' ' May Heaven and
Sylvia grant my suit,' commences one of these
verses, which are full of quaint references to
' wavering hearts, sighing swains, constant
flames,' and such like phrases, unintelligible to
all unacquainted with love. Presently the hated
voice of the call-boy would summon her from
the heaven of her happiness ; when, rising up,
she and Garrick would walk, hand in hand,
towards the wings, in the friendly shades of

which he would kiss her on the lips ; and then, being free of the house, run round to the stage box, that he might be the first to give the signal of her approach by his applause.

Another admirer of Peg Woffington at this period was Sir Charles Hanbury Williams, ' one of the plenipotentiaries of fashion,' wit, satirist, poet, paymaster of the marines, and as pretty a gentleman as ever cracked a bottle at White's. He was the friend of Lady Mary Wortley Montagu, of Fox, of Horace Walpole, and of merry Dick Edgecumbe, and had the reputation of being a rake of the first water. Lady Mary said of him that he might be happy if he added to his natural and acquired endowments a dash of morality ; but Sir Charles knew little of morals and cared for them still less, they being to his mind but dull things at best. However, this lamentable absence of virtue was no drawback to the friendship of his contemporaries, few of whom were a whit better themselves. He could tell the wittiest if not the decentest of stories ; pen a pasquinade in the twinkling of an eye ; ridicule a political enemy in a scathing lampoon ; and gamble from sunset to sunrise ; for all of which qualities he was dear to his friends. With Fox he was ever ' dear Charles ; ' Walpole had his portrait framed in black and gold, and

set in a panel of the bow-window room in that
wonderful gimcrack Gothic castle known as
Strawberry Hill ; whilst Lady Mary hears that
' he suffers under a dearth of flatterers.'   Sir
Charles duly fell in love with the beautiful Woffington, and composed poems addressed to her,
one of which, ' Lovely Peggy,' included in one
of the editions of his works, published in 1776,
was vastly admired by the town.   It is in itself
an excellent example of the love verses of the
period, and is not without touches of poetic
beauty : —

> Once more I 'll tune the vocal shell
> To hills and dales my passion tell,
> A flame which time can never quell,
>   That burns for lovely Peggy.

> Ye greater bards the lyre should hit,
> For say what subject is more fit,
> Than to record the sparkling wit
>   And bloom of lovely Peggy.

> The sun first rising in the morn,
> That paints the dew-bespangled thorn,
> Does not so much the day adorn
>   As does my lovely Peggy.

> And when in Thetis' lap to rest,
> He streaks with gold the ruddy west,
> He 's not so beauteous as undressed
>   Appears my lovely Peggy.

RT. HON. CHARLES JAMES FOX.

Were she arrayed in rustic weed,
With her the bleating flocks I 'd feed,
And pipe upon mine oaken reed.
 To please my lovely Peggy.

With her a cottage would delight,
All 's happy when she 's in my sight,
But when she 's gone it 's endless night,
 All 's dark without my Peggy.

The zephyr air the violet blows,
Or breathes upon the damask rose,
He does not half the sweets disclose
 That does my lovely Peggy.

I stole a kiss the other day,
And trust me, nought but truth I say,
The fragrant breath of blooming May,
 Was not so sweet as Peggy.

While bees from flower to flower shall rove,
And linnets warble through the grove,
Or stately swans the waters love,
 So long shall I love Peggy.

And when death, with his pointed dart,
Shall strike the blow that rives my heart,
My words shall be, when I depart,
 Adieu, my lovely Peggy.

Garrick, as was natural, entertained a great
dread of his verse-making, witty rival, and en-
treated the Woffington not to see or listen to
him. One evening when Garrick visited her,

he asked her how long it was since she had seen
Sir Charles.

' Not for an age,' says she, with a humorous
smile on her charming face.

' Nay,' said Garrick, gravely, ' I know you
have seen him this morning.'

' Well,' replied she, going up to him, her
beautiful lips pouting like a child's, ' I count
time by your absence ; I have not seen you since
morning, and is it not an age since then ? '

CHAPTER VI.

Garrick's Irresolution. — Plays at Ipswich under a False Name.
— First Appearance in Town. — A Memorable Night. —
Description of his Richard. — The Talk of the Town. — Persons of Distinction at the Playhouse. — Our Little Poetical
Hero. — Letters to Peter. — The Wine-merchant will not be
Comforted. — David's Arguments and Fair Promises. — The
Lying Valet. — Mimicking the Old Players. — The Favour
of Great Men. — Going to Dublin with Peg Woffington.

M EANWHILE Garrick continued nervously
irresolute concerning his future, experiencing by turns both hope and despair. Now
his spirits rose at the prospect of his success as
an actor held out to him by his friends and by
the woman he loved ; and again his mind was
sorely depressed by the letters of grave reproof
he received from respectable Peter at Lichfield,
who heard with much disquietude that his brother
David had formed a friendship with one Giffard,
a player. After long-continued mental fluctuations, it happened in the summer of 1741, the
fourth year of his career as a wine-merchant,
that through the interest of this same player and

manager an opportunity was offered him of test-
ing his strength as an actor, and for a few nights
at least, of gratifying the longing and ambition
to play before an audience, which had taken a
firm hold upon his life. Moreover, this could
be done in the most private manner possible, so
that his friends in town, or Peter conducting
his decent business in Lichfield, need know
nothing of the matter ; for the theatre concerning which this offer was made was at Ipswich,
and he could of course change his name for the
occasion.

Accordingly, away he went quite secretly
with Giffard to Ipswich, carrying with him the
Woffington's best wishes for his success; and in
due time he appeared as Aboan, a blackamoor,
in the tragedy of ' Oroonoko,' — a part which
recommended itself to the nervous amateur,
from the fact that the necessary black face
offered an excellent disguise. The reception
he received was sufficient to encourage his appearance in other characters, including that of
Captain Brazen ; and in these his success was
such that the house was not only crowded
nightly by the inhabitants of Ipswich, but the
surrounding gentry drove in their coaches to
see this excellent new player, styling himself
Lyddal. This unlooked-for result, coupled with

the fact of his fast declining business, finally determined him to become an actor; and he accordingly arranged with Giffard to play Richard III.
at his theatre in Goodman's Fields in the coming
autumn. This playhouse, situated in an unsavoury district, had never been favoured with
the company of the polite. Indeed, it merely
existed on sufferance ; four years previously,
the passing of the Licensing Bill had limited
the number of London theatres to two. In
order, therefore, to keep its doors open, the
manager had recourse to a very simple ruse,
which at the same time fulfilled its object ;
this was to charge for an entertainment of
singing and dancing, and perform the plays
gratis. Such was the theatre where Garrick
first made his bow to a London audience. Towards the middle of October it was whispered
in the green-rooms of the two West End theatres, and in the coffee-houses and taverns all
over the town, that a young gentleman of
great promise was about to act the part of
Richard III. in the Goodman's Fields playhouse. Much curiosity therefore obtained,
especially amongst the friends of the said
young gentleman. Presently the ' London
Daily News ' printed the following announcement in its advertising columns : —

GOODMAN'S FIELDS.

At the Late Theatre in Goodman's Fields,
Monday next (Oct. 19th) will be performed a

CONCERT of VOCAL and INSTRUMENTAL MUSIC,

Divided into Two Parts.

Tickets at Three, Two, and One Shilling.

Places for the Boxes to be taken at the Fleece Tavern,
near the Theatre.

N. B. — Between the Two Parts of the Concert will be
presented an Historical Play, call'd The

LIFE AND DEATH OF KING RICHARD THE THIRD.

Containing the Distresses and Death of King Henry VI.,

The Artful Acquisition of the Crown by King Richard,

The Murder of young King Edward V. and his Brother in
the Tower,

The Landing of the Earl of Richmond,

And the Death of King Richard in the Memorable
Battle of Bosworth-Field, being the last that was fought
between the Houses of York and Lancaster,

With many other true Historical Passages.

The Part of King Richard by a Gentleman
(Who never appear'd on any stage).

With entertainments of Dancing, by Mons. Froment,
Mme. Duvall, and the two Masters and Miss Grainer.

DAVID GARRICK.

To which will be added a Ballad Opera in One Act, call'd

THE VIRGIN UNMASKED,

Both which will be performed gratis by Persons for
their Diversion.

The Concert will begin exactly at Six o'clock.

It happened at this very time that a battle
royal was raging between the two greater houses,
where for four consecutive nights ' As You Like
It ' was being played ; Peg Woffington and Milward taking the parts of Rosalind and Orlando
at the Lane, and Mrs. Pritchard and Hale
enacting the same at the Garden.

On the fourth night, Monday, October 19,
1741, Garrick appeared in the part of Richard
III., playing Colley Cibber's freely treated but
very effective version of the great tragedy. In
this the poet laureate, who modelled his style
after an antiquated actor named Sandford, used
in his day to drawl and declaim the part in a
shrill, feeble voice, and strut about the boards,
to the great satisfaction of his audiences. But
nothing could present a more striking contrast
to his playing than that of Garrick's ; here there
was neither strut nor drawl. As he came before
a house crowded by those whom curiosity or
interest had drawn to this end of the town, the
character he assumed was at once visible in the

lines of his singularly mobile face, in t'.e accents of his voice, in every turn and movement of his figure. As he proceeded, it was seen that nature had given place to rant. Here was a man acting as if he veritably felt the contending passions that swayed the wicked king. Never had such playing been seen before, and those who witnessed it were at first undecided as to whether they should accept or reject such a complete innovation. But before they were aware of it he had touched their hearts, and now played upon them at will ; and presently an irresistible burst of applause ringing through the house, proclaimed that his genius had triumphed over prejudice. ' His look, his voice, his attitude changed with every sentiment,' says Arthur Murphy, one of his biographers. ' The rage and rapidity with which he spoke

" The north — what do they in the north,
   When they should serve their sovereign in the west ? "

made a most astonishing impression. His soliloquy in the tent scene discovered the inward man. Everything he described was almost reality ; the spectator thought he heard the hum of either army from camp to camp, and steed threatening steed. When he started from his dream he was a spectacle of horror. In all, the audience saw an exact imitation of Nature.'

Then comes the interesting testimony to his genius of Mr. Swynfen, an honest neighbour and friend of the Garricks at Lichfield, who sat in the Goodman's Fields on this eventful night, and wrote the news of it next day to Peter, preserved in the collection already mentioned. ' My good friend David Garrick performed last night at Goodman's Fields Theatre,' says this good old gentleman. ' I was there, and was witness to a most general applause He gain'd in the character of Richard the Third ; for I believe there was not one in the House that was not in Raptures, and I heard several Men of Judgment declare it their Opinion that nobody ever excelled Him in that Part ; and that they were surprised, with so peculiar a Genius, how it was possible for Him to keep off the stage so long.'

The next day nothing was talked of but the performance of the young gentleman, whose name was not yet printed in the bills, but who was pretty well known to the town. Groups gathered in the coffee-houses to hear the enthusiastic descriptions of him given by those who had witnessed his performance. The critics met each other, exchanged bows, took snuff, bobbed their wigs, raised their eyebrows, and looked grave : for it was certain the world was coming to an end now that the town had ventured to

admire a man in whose favour they had not first
pronounced. To cap all, the ' London Daily
Post,' which had seldom indeed noticed even
the finest performance, actually devoted half a
dozen lines to the commendation of this young
man.

' Last night,' runs the paragraph, ' was perform'd Gratis the Tragedy of Richard III., at
the late Theatre in Goodman's Fields, when the
Character of Richard was perform'd by a Gentleman who never appear'd before, whose reception was the most extraordinary and great that
ever was known upon such an occasion ; and we
hear he obliges the Town this Evening with the
same Performance.'

It was not only the following evening, but
four times during this week, and every night of
the following save one, that he obliged the town
by his performance of Richard. The fame of
his extraordinary acting ran from east to west ;
and every evening a vast concourse of people
gathered outside the doors of the little theatre
hours before they were opened, whilst hundreds
were unable to obtain admittance. Even Drury
Lane, with the acting of the charming Woffington as Adriana in ' The Comedy of Errors,'
Berintha, in ' The Relapse,' and Clarinda, in
' The Double Gallant,' was left half empty.

Time seemed but to increase the fame of this new actor. ' From the polite ends of Westminster,' says Murphy, quaintly enough, ' the most elegant company flocked to Goodman's Fields, insomuch that from Temple Bar the whole way was covered with a string of coaches.' People of the first figure and fashion, dukes and duchesses by the dozen, ministers and members of parliament, wits, critics, and poets, all rushed to see the great actor ; moreover, the Prince was expected nightly. The Rev. Thomas Newton, a gentleman described as a learned person with a critical eye, who afterwards became a right reverend bishop, but who was at this time tutor to Lord Carpenter's son, writes to Garrick to secure for himself and his party a stage box, that they ' might see his looks in the scene with the Lady Anne.' The ladies expressed themselves ' almost in love with Richard,' and Mr. Newton wishes later on to take another box for some other friends, in order to see Garrick in ' The Orphan ' and ' The Lying Valet,' new characters he essayed. These were to include amongst them Mrs. Porter, a famous and most charming actress now some time retired, ' and no less a man than Mr. Pulteney desires to be of our party, and have a place in our box,' writes the Reverend Thomas. Mr. Pulteney was cer-

tainly a man of consequence, having been Secre-
tary of War, and being at this time the most
popular man in England, though in the following
year he 'shrank into insignificance and an
earldom.' For all that, Garrick's arrangements
did not permit him to act in these plays on the
night suggested by the embryo bishop, who
consequently writes to the player, ' It would
certainly have been a very great honour to you,
if of no other advantage, for such a person as
Mr. Pulteney to come so far to be one of
your audience ; and if I had been in your ca-
pacity I should have thought it worth while to
have strained a point, or done almost anything
rather than have disappointed him. I would
have acted that night, if I had spared myself all
the rest for it.'

However, the party came later on, and Mrs.
Porter was in raptures ; ' she returned to town
on purpose to see you,' says Newton, ' and declares she would not but have come for the
world. You are born an actor, she says, and
do more at your first appearing than ever anybody did with twenty years' practice ; and good
God ! says she, what will he be in time ?' Another famous actress, Mrs. Bracegirdle, who
had played in the previous century, and who had
now retired for over thirty years, came out into

the world again, anxious to see this prodigy of her later days ; and with her came old Colley Cibber, who had laughed maliciously whenever Garrick's praises had been sung, but who, when he had seen him act, was forced to mutter the bare admission, ' Why, faith, Bracey, the fellow is clever.'

Among others who flocked to the stuffy little theatre was my Lord Orrery, an authority where the drama was concerned, and a critic, mind you, of the first understanding, and, moreover, a man of vast experience. He was delighted with Garrick's prodigious powers, but feared the young man would be spoiled, ' for,' says his lordship, ' he will have no competitor.' Then his grace of Argyle drove down in his ponderous coach to Goodman's Fields, and swore a ducal oath that this player was superior to the great Betterton of famous memory. Likewise came Horace Walpole, dainty in ruffles and velvet, and high-heeled, silver-buckled shoes, who never had sympathy with public opinions, and now barely admitted with a sneer that ' the wine-merchant turned player ' was an excellent mimic, but he could see nothing in his acting, ' though,' he added, ' it is heresy to say so.' Mr. Pitt came also and added his testimony that ' this young man was the best player in England.'

But amongst all those who came nightly to the playhouse, there was one of whom Garrick was far more proud than the dozen dukes, who, according to Gray, were to be seen at Goodman's Fields of a night. This was none other than Mr. Pope, who was looked upon with the most profound respect, and whose opinions were regarded with feelings little less than reverent by his contemporaries. Garrick, long years after, described his sensations to Percival Stockdale, on learning that the little poet of Twickenham was one of his auditors. 'When I was told,' said he, 'that Pope was in the house, I instantaneously felt a palpitation at my heart; a tumultuous, not a disagreeable emotion in my mind. As I opened my part, I saw our little poetical hero, dressed in black, seated in a side box near the stage, and viewing me with a serious and earnest attention. His look shot and thrilled like lightning through my frame, and I had some hesitation in proceeding from anxiety and from joy. As Richard gradually blazed forth. the House was in a roar of applause, and the conspiring hand of Pope shadowed me with laurels.' The conspiring tongue of little Mr. Pope, however, did him more honour still. Turning to my Lord Orrery — beside whom he was seated — the little poet said, 'That young man never had his equal as an actor, and he will never have a rival ! '

But although the town might ring with the news of his triumph, David had his private misgivings, which were not easily to be overcome, regarding the step he had taken. He knew but too well that his brother Peter, sedate and grave, his sisters, who even in the gentility of their early girlhood had feared to be considered as mere vulgar madams, and his friends — these terrible friends, who are as the plague and pestilence to many an aspiring life — would one and all regard this new departure as a black disgrace wantonly flung upon the spotlessness of their respectability. Accordingly, he must write to them, and get his good friend Mr. Swynfen to do so likewise, and represent in as fair a light as was possible this dreadful act of his, before any false and misleading reports concerning him could reach their ears. On the morning following his great performance, therefore, Mr. Swynfen wrote to Peter ; and even during the excitement of that day David himself found time to pen a letter to his brother, and to his cousin, Peter Fermignac, a scion of the wealthier branch of the family.

'I do not doubt,' commenced Mr. Swynfen, bluntly enough, in his epistle to Peter, 'but you

will soon hear my good Friend David Garrick
performed last night at Goodman's Fields Theatre ; and for fear you should hear any false or
malicious Account that may perhaps be disagreeable to you, I will give you the Truth,
which much pleased me.' Then follows the
account of that most memorable night already
quoted. Moreover, the worthy man strives to
appease Peter by imputing to him sentiments
less narrow in their circumference than those
which sway his neighbours ; which shows that
he mistook his man, as the wine-merchant of
Lichfield soon let him see. ' Many of his
Country Friends,' continues Mr. Swynfen,
' who have been most used to Theatrical Performances in Town Halls, &c., by strollers,
will be apt to imagine the highest Pitch a Man
can arrive at on the Stage is about that exalted
degree of Heroism as the Herberts and the
Hallams have formerly made us laugh and cry
with ; and there are, I don't question, many
others, who because their fathers were call'd
Gentlemen, or perhaps themselves the first, that
will think it a disgrace and a scandal that the
Child of an old Friend should endeavour to
get an honest Livelihood, and is not content
to live in a scanty manner all his Life because
his Father was a Gentleman. I think I know

you well enough to be convinced that you have
not the same sentiments, and I hope there are
some other of his Friends, who will not alter
their Opinion or Regard for Him, till they find
the Stage corrupts his Morals and makes Him
less deserving, which I do not take by any means
to be a necessary consequence, nor likely to
happen to my honest Friend David.'

But honest David's letter to his brother is
not quite so hopeful ; he knows Peter's hard
nature, and pleads to him submissively.

'I rece'd my shirt safe,' he commences, 'and
am now to tell you what I suppose you may
have heard of before this. But before I let
you into my affair, 't is proper to premise some
things, that I may appear less culpable in yr
opinion than I might otherwise do. I have
made an Exact Estimate of my stock of wine,
and what money I have out at interest, and
find that since I have been a wine-merchant I
have run out near four hundred pounds, and
trade not increasing. I was very sensible some
way must be thought of to redeem it. My
mind (as you must know) has been always
inclin'd to ye Stage ; nay, so strongly so that
all my Illness and lowness of Spirits was owing
to my want of resolution to tell you my thoughts
when here. Finding at last both my Inclination

and Interest requir'd some new way of Life, I
have chose ye most agreeable to myself; and
though I know you will be much displeas'd at
me, yet I hope when you shall find that I have
ye genius for an actor without ye vices, you
will think less severe on me, and not be asham'd
to own me for a Brother.' How could Peter
resist this touching appeal? 'Last night,' he
continues, 'I played Richard ye Third to ye
surprise of Every Body; and as I shall make
very near £300 per annum by It, and as it is
really what I doat upon, I am resolv'd to pursue it.' Then he adds nervously, 'Pray write
me an answer immediately,' and concludes with
a postscript: 'I have a farce (" Ye Lying Valet ")
coming out at Drury Lane.'

Then comes the letter to his cousin, Peter
Fermignac. Lest this worthy relative, whom
he is anxious to conciliate, should be appre-
hensive of his design to continue on the stage,
he troubles him with an account of his intention. To him he therefore repeats the excuses
already made to Peter. 'You must know,'
he writes, 'that since I have been in Business
(the wine trade I mean), I have run out almost
half my Fortune.' After some further particu-
lars relative to business, he continues, 'My
mind led me to the stage, which, from being

very young, I found myself very much Inclining
to, and have been very unhappy that I could
not come upon it before. The only thing that
gives me pain is, that my Friends, I suppose,
will look very cool upon me, particularly the
Chief of them ; but what can I do ? I am
wholly bent upon the thing, and can make
£300 per annum by it. As my brother will
settle at Lichfield, I design to throw up the
wine trade as soon as I can conveniently, and
desire you will let my uncle know. If you
should want to speak to me, the Stage Door
will be always open to you, or any other part of
the house ; for I am manager with Mr. Giffard,
and you may always command your most humble servant.'

This letter Mr. Peter Fermignac sent to his
aunt, with the following quaint commentary :
' Dear madam, the under written is a copy of a
Letter sent me from David Garric, who play'd
Crook'd Back Richard last night, and does it
to-night again at Goodman's Fields. I leave
you to consider of it, and am very sorry for the
contents, but I thought fit to communicate them
to you, and am your most dutiful nephew.'

When the sedate Peter had sufficiently recovered from the prodigious blow which his respectable feelings had received by his brother's news,

he wrote up to town, in no gentle terms it may
be assumed. What he said can alone be gathered from David's reply. ' My Dear Brother,'
writes the poor, perplexed player, 'the uneasiness I have received at your letter is inexpres-
sible ; however, 't was a shock I expected, and
had guarded Myself as well as I could against it ;
and the Love I sincerely have for you, together
with ye prevailing Arguments you have made
use of, were enough to overthrow my strongest
resolutions, did not necessity (a very pressing
advocate) on my side convince me that I am
not so much to blame as you think I am. As
to my uncle upbraiding you with keeping our
Circumstances a secret, I am surpris'd at it ;
for to be sure, what I have run out has been
more owing to my own wilfulness than any
Great miscarriage in Trade. But run out I
have, and let me live never so warily, I must
run out more ; and indeed, the Trade we have,
if you will reflect very seriously, can never be
sufficient to maintain me and a servant handsomely. As for the stage,' he urges, with much
meekness of spirit, ' I know in general it deserves your Censure ; but if you will consider
how handsomely and how reputably some have
liv'd, as Booth, Mills. Wilks, Cibber, &c., and
admitted into and admired by the Best Com-

panies, &c. And as my genius that way (by ye best judges) is thought wonderful, how can you be so averse to my proceedings, when not only my Inclinations but my Friends, who at first were surpris'd at my intent by seeing me on ye stage, are now well convinc'd 't was impossible for me to keep off. As to Company,' he continues with a pardonable air of pride, ' ye Best in Town are desirous of mine, and I have rece'd more civilities and favours from such since my playing than I ever did in all my Life before. Mr. Glover (Leonidas, I mean) has been every night to see me, and sent for me, and told me, as well as Every Body he converses with, that he had not seen such acting for ten years before. In short, were I to tell you what they say about me, 't would be too vain, though I am now writing to a Brother. However, Dear Peter, so willing am I to be continu'd in your affections that, were I certain of a less income with more reputation, I would gladly take to It. I have not yet had my name in ye Bills, and have play'd only ye Part of Richard III., which brings crowded audiences every night, and Mr. Giffard returns ye service I have done him very amply. However, Dear Peter, write me a Letter next post, and I 'll give you a full answer, not having Time enough at present. I

have not a Debt of twenty shillings upon me,
so in that be very easy. I am sorry my sisters
are under such uneasiness, and as I really love
both them and you, will ever make it my study
to appear your affectionate Brother.'

But even these soft words had not the desired
effect of turning away Peter's wrath. An honest wine-merchant, whose father had been a
recruiting officer, whose mother had been the
daughter of an impoverished vicar choral, dis-
graced by a brother turned stage-player, was a
serious matter, not to be lightly overlooked.
In the eyes of his neighbours poor Peter must
assuredly fall from the high estate of his respectability ; nay, his very business would assuredly
feel the shock from the proceedings of one who
was once intimately connected with it. Therefore Peter's anger was exceeding great ; the
more so as no persuasion he could use, no
arguments concerning the misfortunes which his
brother's stage-playing must assuredly entail on
the family, had any avail with the perpetrator
of the outrage, who met his complaints with
gentle reasonings, his sneers and murmurings
with fair words and kind.

' I am very sorry you still seem so utterly
averse to what I am so greatly Inclin'd, and to
what ye best Judges think I have ye greatest

of Genius for,' David again writes to him on
the 10th of November. 'The great, nay, inde-
scribable success and approbation I have met
with from ye Greatest Persons in England have
almost made me resolve (though I 'm sorry to
say it against your entreaties) to pursue it, as I
certainly shall make a fortune by it, if Health
continues. Mr. Lyttleton, Mr. Pitt, and several
other members of Parliament were to see me
play Chamont in "Ye Orphan;" and Mr. Pitt,
who is reckon'd ye Greatest Orator in the House
of Commons, said I was ye best actor ye English Stage had produc'd, and he sent a Gentleman to me to let me know he and ye other
Gentlemen would be glad to see Me. The
Prince has heard so great a character of me
that we are in daily expectation of his coming
to same.' Then he proceeds to business, of
which he never lost sight even in his palmiest
days. 'I have been told,' he writes, 'that you
are afraid Giffard has had my money. Upon
my honour, he does not owe me a farthing,
having paid me long ago what I lent him, which
was but £30. I receive at present from him
(tho' 't is a secret) six guineas a week, and am
to have a clear Benefit, which will be very
soon, and I have been offer'd for it £120.
You can't imagine what regard I meet with ;

ye Pit and Boxes are to be put together, and
I shall have all my friends (who still continue
so to me, though you cannot be brought over).
If you come to town, your lodgings will cost
you nothing. I having a bed at Arthur's for you.
Pray let me know if you 'll come immediately.
And if you chuse to have your share with what
you have at Lichfield, ye Cooper shall take a
Strict Survey of ye vaults, and I will be at half
ye expense of ye carriage ; if not, I 'll make
a sale here, but let me know what you resolve upon, and I will assure you 't is my
greatest desire to continue your affectionate
Brother.'

The account of so much honour done the
player by Mr. Glover, an author of eminence
in his day, a clever speaker, and an adviser of
the Prince, and by Mr. Lyttleton, likewise a
friend of His Royal Highness, probably helped
to lighten the burden of disgrace that Peter had
allowed to fall so heavily on his shoulders ; for
David, in writing to him next, says : —

' As you finished your last Letter with saying,
though you did not approve of ye Stage, yet
you would always be my affectionate Brother,
I may now venture to tell you I am very near
quite resolv'd to be a player, as I have ye judgment of ye best Judges (who to a man are of

RICHARD GLOVER ESQ.

opinion) that I shall turn out (nay, they say have) not only ye Best Tragedian, but Comedian in England. I would not say so much to anybody else, but as this may somewhat palliate my Folly you must excuse me. Mr. Lyttleton was with me last night, and took me by the hand, and said he never saw such playing upon ye English stage before. I have great offers from Fleetwood, but he 's going to sell to Gentlemen, and I don't doubt but I will make for myself very greatly. We have greater business than either Drury Lane or Covent Garden. Mr. Giffard himself gave me yesterday twenty Guineas for a Ticket. As to hurting you in your affairs, it shall be my constant endeavours to forward your welfare with my all. If you should want money, and I have it, you shall command my whole, and I know I shall soon be more able by playing and writing to do you service than any other way. My uncle,' he adds, ' I am told, will be reconcil'd to me, for even ye merchants say 'tis an honour to him, not otherwise.'

Surely, with tidings of such prosperity, with offers of such generosity, and with the intelligence of his uncle's reconciliation, Peter could not hold out any longer ; and so a reconciliation ensued, over which the wine-merchant had in after years much reason to rejoice. Meanwhile, David, or as the play-bills down to the 22d of November continued to style him, 'the young gentleman who perform'd Richard,' was playing several new characters, such as Clodio in ' Love Makes a Man,' Chamont in ' The Orphan,' Jack Smatter in ' Pamela,' and winning fresh success. The ' London Daily Post ' of November the 27th, speaking of the Goodman's Fields Playhouse, says : ' Several hundred persons were obliged to return for want of room ; the House being full soon after five o'clock.'

His farce, ' The Lying Valet,' was ready by the end of November, and was produced on the 30th of that month, not at Drury Lane, but at Goodman's Fields, Garrick playing the part of Sharp ; and such was its success, that five days later, the farce, in two acts, was published for a shilling, ' As it is performed Gratis at the late Theatre in Goodman's Fields, by David Garrick ; ' a name to become henceforth memorable in the annals of the stage. Of course a copy of this farce was sent to Peter, with all the pride which an author feels in his first-born. ' On Monday last, I sent you,' he writes to him, ' " The Lying Valet." The Valet takes prodigiously, and is approv'd of by men of Genius, and thought ye most diverting Farce that ever was perform'd. I believe you 'll find it read pretty well, and in performance it 's a general Roar from beginning to end ; and I have got as much Reputation in ye Character of Sharp as in any other character I have perform'd.' Then he names the various plays in which he has acted, thinking Peter would be glad to hear of them, and adds, ' I have had great success in all ; and 't is not determined whether I play tragedy or comedy best. Old Cibber has spoken with ye greatest commendation of my acting.'

On the 2d of December (the occasion of his first benefit), Garrick played this farce, which was preceded by the tragedy of ' The Fair Penitent,' taking the part of Lothario, ' being the first time of his appearance in that character.' So great was the expected crush, it was announced that for this night ' the Stage will be built after the Manner of an Amphitheatre, when servants will be allow'd to keep Places, and likewise in the Front Boxes, but not in the Pit, who are desir'd to be at the House by Three o'clock.'

The downfall of the old school of acting was now complete. Having once seen Nature pourtrayed on the stage, Garrick felt sure the town would never again accept pedantic rant in its place. The old actors were of course terribly

incensed by his success. Quin, who for years
had been without a rival, could ill brook one
now in a novice of five and twenty summers.
The town was, he declared, mad, but would
presently come to its senses, whence, the infer-
ence was, it would return to its old love in the
sturdy person of this famous old ranter again.
The young man's style, he furthermore declared,
was heresy; to which Garrick replied, it was
reformation. He was yet, however, to give the
old school its final blow, by his performance in
' The Rehearsal.' In this amusing comedy —
in which Mr. Bayes, a stage manager, instructs
his company in the way they should act — Garrick saw an ample outlet for the rich vein of
mimicry he possessed, inasmuch that, as the
manager, he could give representations of the
best known actors of the day. Yet for some
time he shrank from affording them such annoy-
ance as this must naturally cause, though Giffard
was desirous of putting the comedy on his stage.
A strange tale, beautifully illustrative of human
nature, hangs thereby, which is told in a manuscript note that I found among the pages of some
old theatrical records, once the property of Dr.
Burney. His son, Charles Burney, writes :

' While Mr. Garrick was acting at the Theatre
in Goodman's Fields, Mr. Giffard, the manager,

urged him to play the part of Bayes on that stage, in order that he might display his talents for mimicry in his imitation of the favourite actors at all the theatres. Mr. Garrick declined it at first; but when Mr. Giffard pressed the point strongly, Mr. Garrick promised to play the part, provided he might be allowed to take off the manager himself. Mr. Giffard declared he had not the slightest objection; but when the trial was made, and Mr. Garrick's imitation of Mr. Giffard created unusual laughter, it offended him so deeply that a challenge was the consequence, and Mr. Garrick was wounded in the arm. This story my father, Dr. Burney, received from Mr. Garrick.'

' The Rehearsal ' was, however, played without the personation of Giffard on the 3d of February, 1742, with prodigious success. The whole town laughed loud and long at the imitations of those they had formerly admired. ' In the character of Bayes,' says Arthur Murphy, ' he exhibited to the life the vain coxcomb who had the highest conceit of himself, and thought the art of dramatic poetry consisted in strokes of surprise and thundering versification. The players of his day he saw were equally mistaken. In order, therefore, to display their errors in the most glaring light, he took upon him occa-

sionally to check the performers who were re-
hearsing his play, and teach them to deliver
their speech in what he called the true theatrical
manner. For this purpose he selected some of
the most eminent performers of the time, and by
his wonderful powers of mimicry was able to
assume the air, the manner, and the deportment
of each in his turn. Delane was at the head of
his profession. He was tall and comely, had a
clear and strong voice, but was a mere declaimer.
Garrick began with him ; he retired to the upper
part of the stage, and drawing his left arm across
his breast, rested his right elbow on it, raising a
finger to his nose, and then came forward in a
stately gait, nodding his head as he advanced,
and in the exact tones of Delane spoke the following lines : —

> " So boar and sow, when any storm is nigh,
>   Snuff up and smell it gath'ring in the sky." '

Those who were mimicked were of course
outrageous, but the town was highly diverted,
and Garrick and his manager were equally satisfied. In March he had another benefit, on the
18th, when he played Master Johnny, a lad of
fifteen, in ' The School-boy,' after the performance of ' King Lear.' ' The farce of " The
School-boy," ' says Boaden, in his biographical
memoir, ' was written by Colley Cibber, who

was still living ; and he might, and very probably did, see that wonderful junction of eighty-
four and fifteen by the same actor.' His fame
daily increased, the crowds still flocked to Goodman's Fields, and the great ones of the earth
paid him honour. In April he writes to Peter
with a sense of triumph at his heart, —

' Ye favour I meet from ye Greatest Men,
has made me far from Repenting of my choice.
I am very intimate with Mr. Glover, who will
bring out a tragedy next winter upon my account. I have supped twice with ye Great
Mr. Murray, Counsellor, and shall with Mr.
Pope by his introduction. I supped with Mr.
Lyttleton, ye Prince's Favourite, last Thursday
night, and met with ye highest civility and com-
plaisance. He told me he never knew what
acting was till I appeared, and said I was only
born to act what Shakespeare writ. These
things daily occurring give me great Pleasure.
I dined with Lord Halifax and Lord Sandwich,
two very ingenious noblemen, yesterday, and
am to dine at Lord Halifax's next Sunday with
Lord Chesterfield. I have ye pleasure of being very intimate with Mr. Hawkins Browne
of Burton ; in short, I believe nobody (as an
actor) was ever more caressed, and my character as a private man makes them more desir-

ous of my company. All this *entre nous* as one
brother to another. I am not fix'd for next
year, but shall certainly be at ye other end of
ye Town. I am offered five hundred guineas
and a clear benefit, or part of management. I
can't be resolved what I shall do till ye season
is finished.'

In this month he made his first appearance at
Drury Lane, on which occasion he played for
the benefit of the widow of a comedian named
Harper ; and later on entered into an engagement
with Fleetwood to play at his theatre in the
coming autumn. Before the end of this most
memorable season, his fame had spread so far
that it crossed the St. George's Channel, and
Du Val, the manager of Smock Alley Theatre
in Dublin, arranged with him and Peg Woffington to play in that fair city in the months of
June, July, and August. And so together they
departed for Ireland.

CHAPTER VII.

Excitement in Dublin. — A Warm Greeting. — The Delight of the Town. — Hamlet and Ophelia. — Back to London. — The Rival Playhouse. — Quin's Reputation. — His Contempt for Garrick. — Quin and Macklin. — A Green-room Quarrel. — Making it up. — Charming Susanna Cibber. — 'A Romp and a Good-natured Boy.' — Theo Cibber's Baseness. — Elopement, Rescue, and Action. — Legal Bathos. — Woffington and Garrick at Drury Lane.

THE announcement that Peg Woffington, a child of the people, who had thirteen years ago sung in a canvas booth in George's Court, had first put forth her genius at the Aungier Street playhouse, and had since gained widespread fame in London town, was to appear at the Smock Alley Theatre, threw the excitable citizens of Dublin into a fever of delight. This was heightened by the advertisements stating that Garrick would likewise play on the same stage at the same time. The season was not to commence at Smock Alley till the middle of June. On the 8th of that month the *Dublin Mercury* announced to its readers that 'the famous Mr. Garrick and Miss Woffington are

hourly expected from England to entertain the
nobility and gentry during the summer season,
when especially the part of Sir Harry Wildair
will be performed by Miss Woffington.' The
same journal, it may be noticed, requested the
manager of the theatre 'that he will cause the
nails to be carefully pulled out of the benches
of the pit, otherwise nine gentlemen in ten
will be a pair of stockings out of pocket every
time they go there.'

On the 11th of June, 1742, Peg Woffington
arrived in her native city with Garrick and the
Signora Barbarina, who was to dance between
the acts, and represent in her charming person
a Nymph of the Plain, in the new grand ballet
called 'The Rural Assembly.'   Dancing, it may
be here remarked, was an important item in the
programme during this engagement ; for presently, when, at the desire of several persons
of quality, Garrick played the part of Lothario
in 'The Fair Penitent,' the following ' entertainments of dancing ' were given between the
acts.   At the conclusion of Act I., ' The Grecian Sailor,' by Mr. Will Delamain ; of Act II.,
' The Wooden Shoe Dance,' by Mr. Morris ;
of Act III., a musett by Signora Barbarina ; of
Act IV., ' The Old Woman with Pierrot in the
Basket,' by Mr. Morris.

Four days after the arrival of the Woffington
and Garrick, the season commenced at the
Smock Alley playhouse, when she appeared in
her famous character as Sir Harry Wildair.
Her name had become a familiar sound in the
mouths of the goodly citizens; stories of her
wit and repartee were yet recounted in the quad-
rangles of Trinity College; and a tradition of
her beauty lingered like a warm memory in the
hearts of a people never insensible to the effect of woman's loveliness. She had come back
to her own people; not a man and woman in
the town but felt as if they had a special interest in her; as if her triumphs in some way
reflected credit on them in whose midst the
first years of her life had been spent. So the
audience that gathered to receive her on this
the first night of her reappearance was great.
As she came upon the stage, she saw a sea
of bright faces beaming on her from pit to gallery; and a pleasant sense of kindly gratitude
went out from her heart to theirs that united
them in a common bond of friendship. Cheer
upon cheer rang through the house, in response
to which, with a strange fluttering at her heart,
with smiles on her lips, and with tears in her
beautiful eyes, she bowed again and again.
Garrick was not playing that night, but he

stood at the wings to witness her reception, and when she came off the stage he was ready to greet her. ' Ah ! Peggy,' he said, ' you are the queen of all hearts.' She looked straight at the bright face before her, and a smile in which sadness lurked shadow-like came on her lips. ' Ay,' she replied, as she passed him, ' queen of all hearts, yet not legal mistress of one.'

Dublin audiences had pleasant memories of her Sir Harry Wildair, but practice having added a higher polish, a more subtle finish to her acting, they were now delighted beyond expression with the perfect picture of the graceful and accomplished rake which she presented them. She became the theme of every tongue ; prints of her were exposed for sale in the stationers' windows ; and ballads setting forth the charms of ' purty Peggy, the true love of my heart, with eyes as black as hurtle-berry, and glance like Cupid's dart,' were sung and sold in vast numbers in the streets.

On the third night of the season, Garrick appeared as Richard the Third, the Woffington playing Lady Anne, and the theatre was again crowded to excess by people of the first consequence, who three hours before the performance commenced had sent servants to keep their

GARRICK AS HAMLET.

places. The combination of two such famous personages playing in the same house made the town stage-mad ; and the scenes which were occasionally witnessed in the playhouse were distressing. Women shrieked at Richard's death, sobbed aloud at sad Ophelia's madness, and went into hysterics over the sorrows of King Lear. The heat which the people endured in the sti-fling atmosphere for hours was prodigious. So warm was the season towards the end of June and the commencement of the following month, that the ' Dublin Mercury ' of July the 6th mentions that ' oats is very near being reaped, and if the weather is favourable we will have some in our own market next Saturday ; which is something extraordinary, oats being the latest grain.' The result of this unusually warm weath-er and the crowded houses in Smock Alley was, that a fever broke out in the town, which at-tacked many, and carried away numbers from the playhouse to the grave.

It was during this engagement that Garrick first attempted the part of Hamlet, which he had long and carefully studied. The Dublin citizens were not only enthusiastic admirers of the drama, but were, moreover, profound wor-shippers of Shakespeare ; therefore the an-nouncement that Garrick was about to play

this favourite character gave them unbounded
satisfaction, and though their expectations were
great, they were not disappointed. Never had
they witnessed such acting. On his first appearance the marked melancholy of his face, the
deep thought dwelling in his eyes, his listless
movements, and attitudes indicative of depres-
sion struck all beholders ; while his mere utter-
ance of the line, ' I have that within me which
passeth all show,' sent a thrill of sympathy
through their hearts. When presently the ghost
appeared, the colour fled from his face, the
words trembled as they escaped his lips. Then
his exquisite sensibility, the melting tenderness
of his love for Ophelia, the whirlwind of his
passion, the depth and despair of his grief, were
pourtrayed with an effect never before produced. ' The strong intelligence of his eye,'
says Davis, speaking of him in this play, ' the
animated expression of his whole countenance,
the flexibility of his voice, and his spirited action
riveted the attention of an admiring audience.'
Nothing could be more graceful, more pathetic,
more beautiful than the Woffington as Ophelia ;
her love and sorrow were inexpressibly tender, her madness filled the house with awe and
brought tears to many eyes. But whether she
played Ophelia or Cordelia, Lætitia in ' The

Old Bachelor' or Miss Lucy in 'The Virgin
Unmasked,' she charmed her Dublin admirers.

On the first night of July she took her benefit, when was presented 'The Tragical History
of King Richard the Third ; the part of King
Richard to be performed by Mr. Garrick, being
the last time of his appearing in that character
during the season ; the part of Lady Anne to
be performed by Miss Woffington ; with entertainments of dancing by Signora Barbarina.
To which will be added a diverting ballad opera
called " The Virgin Unmasked." The part of
Miss Lucy by Miss Woffington, with a new
epilogue in the character of Miss Lucy wrote
by Mr. Garrick.' This brief but remarkable
season ended on the 19th of August, 1742,
when the Woffington and Garrick returned to
London, preparatory to their appearance in
September at old Drury Lane.

The London season now commencing was
one of the most brilliant and memorable in the
history of the stage, — brilliant because of those
two stars who had so suddenly arisen in the
theatrical firmament ; memorable as a period
when the battle between the old school and the
new was fought, with a vast show of bravery
on either side. At Drury Lane, Fleetwood had
gathered round him, besides the Woffington and

Garrick, such favourite players as Kitty Clive,
Mrs. Pritchard, and Macklin; whilst at Covent
Garden were Mrs. Cibber, Quin, Ryan, and
Bridgewater. Quin was the acknowledged
head of the old school. He had in his day
played with Wilks and Booth, and since the re-
tirement of the latter he had no rival till young
Garrick came to push him from his high place
in the playgoers' regard. His famous soliloquy
in Cato, it was remembered, had been encored;
his Sir John Bute had been pronounced inimitable, his Falstaff was considered unequalled.
Foote recommended any one who wanted to
witness a character perfectly played to see Mr.
Quin in this part; 'and if he does not express
a desire to spend an evening with that merry
mortal,' said the wit, 'why, I would not spend
one with him, if he would pay my reckoning.'
Quin's contempt for Garrick and his new-
fangled ways was openly avowed. 'If he is
right,' said the veteran, with an incredulous
smile, 'then I and the rest of the players must
have been wrong.' He had no fear, therefore,
of this young jackanapes, and was ready to
test the public favour with him any night.

The dislike which he cherished for Garrick
he likewise heartily extended to another member of the Drury Lane company, — Macklin,

who by his playing the part of Shylock in a
realistic manner but a little before, had, it was
certain, paved the way for the natural school of
acting. Moreover, there had been an old standing quarrel between these actors, the origin of
which happily illustrates the manners of the
green-room in those days. It happened one
night that, when Macklin was playing the part
of Jerry Blackacre to Quin's Captain Manly,
the former, by some business he introduced,
made the audience laugh heartily. When they
came off the stage, Quin, who ruled as supreme
despot in the theatre, abused him in round
terms, told him he was at his tricks, and there
was no having a chaste scene with him as an
actor. To this Macklin replied that he did not
want to disturb him, but was anxious to show
off a little himself. In the following scenes
Macklin continued the same business, when
the audience now laughed more than ever, and
gave him some signs of their approbation; which
disturbed the great man mightily, who, on going
into the green-room, indulged in fresh abuse.
Macklin declared he could not play otherwise ;
Quin insisted that he could, to which the other
replied in plain English, ' You lie ! ' Now at
that instant it happened that Quin was chewing
an apple, which in his vast indignation he spat

into his hand and flung full in Macklin's face.
In a second the green-room was in confusion;
there was a violent scuffle, and in less than a
. minute Macklin had forced Quin into a chair
and was pummelling his face in a right hearty
manner, until it was swelled to double its ordinary size. To make matters worse, Quin was
obliged to go on the stage in a short time, but
he mumbled his part in such a manner that the
audience began to hiss; whereupon he at once
stepped to the centre, informed them that something unpleasant had happened, and that he
was ill.

When the curtain was down, he told Macklin he must give him satisfaction, and that when
he had changed his clothes he would wait for
him at the Obelisk at Covent Garden. Macklin promised he would be with him presently;
but when Quin had gone he remembered he
had to play in the after piece, so he resolved
that till this was over he would let Quin fret
and fume. When the part was finished, Fleetwood, who was desirous of peace among the
members of his company, carried Macklin to his
house, where he made him sup and sleep, and,
when morning came, persuaded him to make an
apology to Mr. Quin, which he did, and there
the matter dropped. After this no word was

MR. QUIN

spoken between them for long, and a studied
deportment on either side seemed to indicate
that nothing save the necessity of business could
ever make them associate again ; till at last it
happened they both, in company with many
others, met one evening in a tavern at Covent
Garden. Their hearts were softened, for they
had just returned from laying a fellow actor at
rest, — an excellent fellow, the son of a baker,
concerning whom Foote, who could not resist
being funny even on such an occasion, said
they ' had been to see him shovelled into the
family oven.' By degrees the company at the
tavern dropped off one by one, until these two
were left together.

Presently Quin roused himself, looked round,
and finding he was alone in Macklin's company,
became embarrassed ; and for some moments
there was silence in the room. But in a little
while he, in polite and solid phrases, drank
Macklin's health, which the latter, as in duty
bound, returned. Then came a pause more
awkward than the first, which Quin again broke
by addressing his companion. ' There has been
a foolish quarrel between you and me, sir,' said
he, ' which, though accommodated, I must con-
fess I have been unable to forget till now. The
melancholy occasion of our meeting, and the

I. — II

circumstance of our being left together, I thank
God, have made me see my error. If you can,
therefore, forget it, give me your hand, and let
us live together in future like brother performers.' Macklin eagerly stretched out his hand,
and assured him of his friendship in hearty
words. It would not have been proper if this
reconciliation was not sealed by a fresh bottle,
ordered by Macklin, which was followed by
another called for by Quin ; and by the time
this was finished, the latter had quietly closed
his eyes on this wicked world of hatred and
quarrels and revenge, and wandered into the
peaceful land of dreams. The light of early
dawn had by this time begun to peep in at the
high, narrow windows of the tavern parlour ;
the candles burned low in their sockets, and it
was full time for Mr. Quin to rest in his virtuous bed. A chair was therefore sent for, but
not one could be found at that hour, when
Macklin, desiring the waiters to lift the great
man on his back, carried him in that manner to
his lodgings. But Quin was not, in his cooler
moments, ready to act up to the words he had
uttered when his heart and his head were softened by wine. He seldom mentioned Macklin's name without a sneer or a sarcastic remark ;
and he was now mortified that this excellent old

actor should strengthen the opposition company of Drury Lane playhouse.

The actress engaged to take the principal female parts at Covent Garden was the wife of the unfortunate scapegrace Theophilus Cibber. This lady, who rejoiced in the name of Susanna Maria, long occupied the attention of the town. She was the daughter of a respectable upholsterer in Covent Garden, and sister to Thomas Arne, afterwards doctor of music. She, too, had a musical genius, and a voice so sweet that Handel specially arranged one of the airs in the ' Messiah ' to suit her. Shortly after her marriage with Theo Cibber she expressed a strong desire to become an actress, for which her melodious voice, beautiful face, and graceful figure seemed eminently suited. She therefore received instructions from her father-in-law, old Colley, who was regarded as a master of his art. She subsequently appeared as Zara in the tragedy of that name at Drury Lane in the year 1736, when, according to a quaint account, ' she gave both surprise and delight to the audience, who were no less charmed with the beauties of her present performance than with the prospect of future entertainment from so valuable an acquisition to the stage, — a prospect which was ever after perfectly maintained, and a meridian lustre shone forth fully equal to what was promised from the morning dawn.'

The ' meridian lustre ' was for a time, however, eclipsed by the ugly shadow of her husband's wickedness ; the story of which vastly diverted the town, whilst it lent additional interest in the performances of this frail and beautiful woman, who was more sinned against than sinning. Theophilus Cibber had, even in the first years of their married life, appropriated his wife's earnings, and freely squandered them in reckless profligacy. Not satisfied, however, with this, he being sorely pressed for money by reason of his extravagances, and being utterly devoid of principle, determined to sell his wife's honour. For this purpose Mr. Cibber, hideous and worthless, introduced to her house a young gentleman of comely mien, who was possessed of station and fortune. The young gentleman's name was William Sloper ; but Cibber presented him as Mr. Benefit, adding that the youth ' was a romp and a good-natured boy.' Soon after Mrs. Cibber making the acquaintance of Sloper, her spouse, affectionately anxious to give her change of air, took lodgings at Kensington for her and himself and the young gentleman, whose good-nature Mr. Cibber tested by borrowing

MRS. CIBBER.

from him sums amounting to four hundred pounds. They had been but a little while established at Kensington when, unfortunately, Mr. Cibber found himself called away on pressing business to France. When he subsequently returned, he refused to occupy his former lodgings, but was obliging enough to hire a bed for himself at the Blue Green Inn, not far removed. When he had first supped comfortably with his wife and their mutual friend, he retired nightly to this inn, being conducted thither by a man with a lanthorn and a candle. Next morning he returned to breakfast with them. For the accommodations, both at the lodgings and the inn, young Sloper freely paid, being a good-natured boy, and, moreover, a romp.

Now Mrs. Cibber, seeing her husband's baseness, despised him heartily, and was too spirited to admit of an arrangement by which her lover was heavily mulcted of his money, whilst her infamous spouse was spared the censure of the world. She therefore eloped with Sloper, whom she had learned to love. This was a movement Mr. Cibber had not expected, and it was now plain to him that he must pose before the town as an outraged husband whose friendship had been vilely abused. The *rôle* has frequently

been played since then with more or less success. He therefore, accompanied by Mr. Fife,
a sergeant in the Guards, set off in a coach for
Burnham, the place where Sloper was staying,
in order to rescue his wife. Entering her lodgings whilst she and her friend were at breakfast,
Cibber and the sergeant of the Guards carried
her away, whilst Sloper cursed many oaths and
called Theophilus a villain. As she was being
taken to the coach, her lover walking beside her,
she put her hand in her pocket and gave him a
watch, on which he cried out 't was well remembered, as the rascal would have had it else.
When they came to the inn at Slough, Cibber
and his wife rested there, and next day he drove
her across country, fearing she might be rescued
by her lover, and, entering the town next evening, he placed her at the ' Bull Head Tavern,'
near Clare Market, under the care of Mr. Stint,
candle-snuffer at Covent Garden playhouse.
Presently her brother, Mr. Arne, came, and he
called out to Mr. Stint, and besought him to let
his sister go with him, saying he would take care
of her ; but the candle-snuffer refused, making
answer, ' I shall not betray the trust which was
placed in me.' Then, not being admitted, Arne
gathered together a great crowd from the neighbouring market, to the number of over one hun-

dred, and broke into the house, and beat the snuffer of candles severely, injuring him in the body, and tearing the clothes from his back, which was left naked. In this manner Mrs. Cibber was rescued and restored to her friend, under whose protection and care she lived happily till her death.

Cibber, seeing in this a cause for the recovery of damages, took an action against Sloper for eloping with his wife, whereby he, sad to relate, 'lost her company, comfort, society, and assistance.' The damages claimed for such loss were estimated at the round sum of five thousand pounds. The foolish bathos indulged in by the gentlemen learned in the law who conducted the case is quite on a par with that which distinguishes many members of that eminent profession at the present day. The wise Solicitor General, one Mr. Strange, who stated the plaintiff's case, declared in a voice choked by emotion that no sum of money could compensate for the injury done to Mr. Cibber, which was of the most tender concern to his peace of mind, happiness, and hopes of posterity ; for no sum of money could restore that tranquillity of mind which had now deserted him forever. The learned Mr. Strange, however, took an opportunity of hinting that five thousand pounds

would be regarded by his client as a slight rec-
ompense to his deeply wounded honour. The
observations ' upon the plaintiff being a player,'
made by the eloquent gentleman, are wonderfully quaint, and moreover amusing, when read
by the light of modern times. He was fully
aware that in a matter of this nature ' players
were considered as not upon the same footing
with the rest of the subjects.' It was true the
plaintiff was a player, *but* he was also a gentleman, being well descended and having had a
liberal education ; his father was well known to
all gentlemen who delighted in theatrical entertainments to be of the first figure in that profession, and an author too ; and the plaintiff's
grandfather was the best statuary of his times ;
and the plaintiff, by the mother's side, was
related to William of Wykeham, and in right of
that pedigree had received his education upon
a foundation of government. The learned gentleman likewise dwelt upon Mr. Cibber being
' endowed with the finest sense of morality,'
and became eloquent on the mischievous consequences of suffering a man to commit such an
injury to the married state without being obliged
to repair it in damages. The jury, however, duly
appreciated Mr. Cibber's fine sense of morality
and Mr. Strange's bathos, and awarded ten

pounds damages to the ill-looking vagabond, Theophilus Cibber.

On the 22d of September, 1742, Covent Garden Theatre opened for the season with 'Othello,' Mrs. Cibber playing Desdemona, — it being ' her first appearance on that stage.' The parts were ·all new dressed and the theatre new decorated,' as the bills informed the public. A few nights later, Peg Woffington and Garrick appeared respectively as Sylvia and Captain Plume, and so great a crowd was expected that it was announced ' No persons will be admitted behind the scenes but those who have silver tickets.' The lines of carriages and chairs which had stretched from Temple Bar to Whitechapel when Garrick had played at Goodman's Fields, now blocked up Drury Lane and its adjacent streets. Night after night the theatre was crowded to excess, and nothing could exceed the delight and applause when the two reigning favourites appeared in the one piece. It became plain even to Quin, who still thundered and strutted at Covent Garden, that the days of the old school were numbered. Yet he was not willing to quietly lay down his arms and own himself defeated in the combat with this young David, but plucked up courage enough to play Richard the Third on the same night as Garrick.

An account of the marked difference between
the champion of the old school and the new is
given us by one who saw both play later on in
Rowe's ' Fair Penitent,' on the stage of Drury
·Lane.　Garrick took the part of Lothario, Quin
of Horatio.　Upon the rising of the curtain the
latter presented himself in a green velvet coat
embroidered down the seams, an enormous full-
bottomed periwig, rolled stockings, and high-
heeled square-toed shoes. ' With very little
variation of cadence, and in a deep, full tone,
accompanied by a sawing kind of action, which
had more of the senate than of the stage in it,
he rolled out his heroics, with an air of dignified
indifference which seemed to disdain the plaudits
that were bestowed on him,' writes Richard
Cumberland in his ' Memoirs.' ' But when I
beheld little Garrick, young and light, and alive
in every muscle and in every feature, Heavens !
what a transition !　It seemed as if a whole
century had been stept over in the transition of
a single scene ; old things were done away, and
a new order at once brought forward, bright and
luminous, and clearly destined to dispel the bar-
barisms and bigotry of a tasteless age, too long
attached to the prejudices of custom, and super-
stitiously devoted to the illusions of imposing
declamation.'

Early in this season Garrick produced ' King Lear,' which he had attempted at Goodman's Fields, and subsequently played during his Dublin engagement. As an instance of the pains which he took in the study of his characters, it may be mentioned that when he first played in this tragedy he had requested his old friend Macklin, and Dr. Barrowly, a physician by profession, a dramatic critic by reputation, to sit in judgment on his performance. These worthy men accepted the pleasurable task, and with that conscientiousness which distinguishes friends delivered their opinions next morning. He was dressed very appropriately for King Lear, they admitted, but he did not sufficiently enter into the infirmities of a man fourscore and upwards. Then in the repetition of the curse he began too low and ended too high, the reverse of which would, they argued, have a better effect ; and in the fourth act he had not dignity enough, and his voice was too loud. To all of which Garrick listened with patience, nay, he even made notes of their remarks, and, thanking them, said he would not again play the part till he had profited by their judicious hints. When in due time he again appeared as King Lear, his friends, who once more acted as his critics, assured him he played the part rather worse

than before. They were good enough to offer
him their services at rehearsal, which he declined
on the plea that so much graciousness would
embarrass him. On his third appearance as the
sad old man his critics were of opinion that he
had sufficiently profited by their advice, and
praised him accordingly. The announcement
that he was again to play the part with the
Woffington as Cordelia caused a thrill of excitement in every coffee-house and tavern in
town ; nor on the night when the Drury Lane
curtain fell on the last act of the tragedy was
his audience disappointed.

O'Keeffe tells us his exclaiming, in the bitterness of his anger, ' I will do such things — what
they are I know not,' and his sudden recollec-
tion of his own want of power were so pitiable
as to touch the heart of every spectator. The
simplicity of his saying, ' Be these tears wet —
yes, faith,' putting his finger to the cheek of
Cordelia, was exquisite. Never had the sorrows, rage, and madness of the king been so
pourtrayed, and never had Garrick more forcibly
impressed the public. ' The curse,' says Macklin, ' exceeded all imagination, and had such an
effect that it seemed to electrify the audience
with horror. The words " kill — kill — kill,"
echoed all the revenge of the frantic king, whilst

he exhibited such a sense of the pathetic on dis-
covering Cordelia as drew tears of commisera-
tion from the whole house. In short, he made
it a *chef-d'œuvre*, and a *chef-d'œuvre* it continued
to the end of his life.' Garrick had carefully
studied the expressions and signs of madness
which he so skilfully represented from one who
had suddenly lost his reason through a dreadful
affliction. This unhappy man had, whilst dan-
dling his only child, a little girl of whom he
was passionately fond, at his dining-room window, let it drop into the flagged area, when it
was instantly killed. His shrieks summoned
the household, who, by way of assuaging his
grief, placed the lifeless body of the child in his
arms. From that moment his senses fled forever. But for years he almost daily rehearsed
the terrible tragedy ; seizing a pillow, he would
dandle and caress it, then let it suddenly drop,
when he gave vent to the most heart-piercing
shrieks, which gradually subsided to low, tremu-
lous moans. From this study Garrick had taken
his hints for the representation of King Lear's
madness over the body of Cordelia which had
electrified his audience.

CHAPTER VIII.

Peg Woffington and Garrick keep House. — Old Colley Cibber.
— Drinking Tea at Peggy's Rooms. — Fielding, Quin, Mrs.
Porter, Foote, Johnson, and Macklin. — The Woffington
and Garrick part. — Polly Woffington, Lord Tyrawley's
Amour. — George Anne Bellamy. — Acting in a Barn. —
Captain Cholmondeley's Marriage. — Violette the Dancer.
— Her Love for Garrick. — Marriage. — Peg Woffington
goes to Covent Garden. — Her Dublin Engagement.

ON their return from Dublin, Peg Woffington
and Garrick kept house together in Bow
Street, when it was agreed between them that
they should alternately defray the monthly expenses.   Here they entertained the first wits
of the day, and it soon became a standing joke
that a more hospitable board was always spread
before their visitors on the month when it was
Peggy's turn to pay the reckoning. What illustrious men and women, whose names are now
as household words in our mouths, assembled
in her rooms ; what wit and repartee were exchanged round her board ! Here came Samuel
Foote, the prince of wits, the most perfect of
mimics, whom Garrick feared in secret, and
conciliated in public ; and burly-figured Samuel

Johnson, now a writer for the 'Gentleman's
Magazine,' who likewise feared Foote, but
chuckled heartily over the jokes he made at
Davy's expense ; and Charles Macklin, who
had always an excellent story to tell, and told
it with the humour native to his race; and Mrs.
Porter, who had played to Queen Anne, and
who now delighted in meeting the young generation of players who were carrying the town
before them ; and Henry Fielding, who just at
this time had produced his comedy ' The Wedding Day,' with but little success. And likewise came Dr. John Hoadly (son of the right
reverend bishop), a chaplain in the household
of the Prince of Wales, and, as became one
who held such position, a play-writer. It was
here, in the Woffington's lodgings, as he mentions in his letters, that he read Garrick his
farce, 'The Force of Truth.' Another playwright also frequently visited these pleasant
apartments in Bow Street, — old Colley Cibber,
an antiquated beau, dramatic author, retired
player, ex-manager, and most execrable laureate, at your service. Watch him as he enters
Garrick's lodgings ; his ponderous wig falls
upon the shoulders of his velvet coat, richly
embroidered at the seams and at the flaps ; his
shrunken shanks are clad in silken stockings ;

his feet encased in high-heeled, silver-buckled
shoes ; his thin fingers are adorned with precious stones ; and as he presses his gold-laced
hat above his heart and makes a low bow to
Mistress Woffington, with whom 't is whispered
he is in love, there is a world of grace in his
movements. His thin sharp features, aquiline
nose, bright small eyes, and great plumage-like
wig, together with his solemn, strutting air, give
him the appearance of some grotesque bird
at once venerable and vindictive looking.
Amongst all the actors of the old school there
is not one so slow to admit the merits of Garrick's powers, and old Colley's sharpest words
are continually hurled at young Davy's head.

Let us picture to ourselves a few of the Woffington's friends — Ryan, Fielding, Mrs. Porter,
and of course Cibber and Garrick — drinking
tea in Peggy's sitting-room in Bow Street ;
a high-ceilinged, wainscoted apartment, with
quaint engravings and concave mirrors hanging on the painted walls, silver sconces branching from the carved oak chimney-piece, and a
polished floor on which the high heels of the
company patter when they walk. Let us listen
to their pleasant banter, their wit, their friendly
bickerings and droll stories.

'Faith, I 'm vastly sorry,' says old Cibber,

HENRY FIELDING, ÆTATIS XLVIII.

with a wicked twinkle in his eye that belies
his words addressed to Fielding, 'that your
" Wedding Day " did n't bring you more pleasure and profit.'

' Much obliged to you, Mr. Cibber,' says the
unsuccessful dramatist, ' but the public taste
has been spoiled for originality by the plagiarised rubbish forced down its throat for the last
fifty years.'

' Ha, ha, ha ! ' laughs burly Quin, ' that 's
one for you, Mr. Cibber.'

The laureate drew out his box and daintily
helped himself to a pinch of snuff.

' When,' said Garrick, by way of soothing
him, ' may we hope to have another comedy
from Mr. Cibber's pen ? '

' Psh ! ' said the old man, spitefully, throwing
away the snuff he held in his dainty fingers,
' what is the use of my writing another comedy,
when we have no actors to play it ? ' [1]

' It would be impossible, indeed, sir,' said
Garrick, with a malicious smile hovering on his
lips, ' to get actors to play such absurd characters
as " The Rival Fools." ' — This was a comedy
of Cibber's which had been a dead failure, and
he now winced at its name, whilst the others
laughed with a pleasant sense of enjoyment.

[1] Macklin's ' Memoirs,' p. 101.

' Now,' said the charming hostess from behind her tea-kettle, ' this is my kingdom, and here I rule supreme — '

' Madame,' said Cibber, rising from his high-backed chair, and bowing to her with courtly grace, — ' Madame, you rule supreme in all hearts.'

' Much obliged to you, sir,' said Peg, with one of her brightest smiles, ' but I was about to say that I won't have my subjects quarrel among themselves. We poor players are looked upon by one half the world as rogues and vaga-bonds, and by the other half as soulless pup-pets ; why can we not regard each other with kindness ? '

'True, ma'am,' says Mrs. Porter, her wrinkled face beaming all over with kindness.

' Speaking of puppets,' said Ryan, in his whistling voice, ' I 'll tell you a story — '

' Ah, you often tell stories, Jimmy,' said Garrick.

' A story of the great Betterton,' continued Ryan, unheeding the interruption. ' One day, being in company with a rustic at Bartholomew Fair, he went to visit the puppet-show. The manager refused to take the money. " Mr. Betterton," says he, " you are a fellow actor ; walk in and see my company perform, and wel-

come, sir." The rustic, who had never before
been within a booth or playhouse, expressed
himself vastly delighted by the humour of the
puppets. "Faith," he says, "they are such
jolly fellows, I will drink with them." Betterton assured him they were but rags and sticks;
but this the rustic refused to believe till he was
taken behind the scenes, and saw the once
merry company silent now, and laid pell-mell in
a box. On that same night Betterton took him
to the theatre, and placed him in front of the
stage, by way of giving him a great treat, as he
and Mrs. Barry were to play in "The Orphan;"
and, thought Betterton, if the fellow was amazed
by the performance of puppets, how much more
will he delight in good actors. When the play
was over, Betterton met his friend. "Well,"
says he, "how liked you the entertainment?"
"I don't know," replies Hodge; "but 't was
well enough for rags and sticks." '

'Gad!' said Garrick, 'the opinion of the
rustic and of the great Mr. Johnson about us
are much the same. What did he say the other
day?' (and Garrick drew down his wig on his
forehead, wrinkled up his face in an inimitable
manner, and mimicked Johnson's voice to perfection), ' "a player, sir, is a fellow who claps a
hump on his back, and a lump on his leg, and

cries, ' I am Richard III.' Nay, sir, a ballad-
singer is a higher man, for he does two things ;
he repeats and he sings, there is both recitation
and music in his performance ; the player only
recites." ' [1]

When they had all laughed at Garrick's imitation : ' Egad,' says Quin, ' I 'll tell you what
Lord Lincoln said to me the other day. " Quin,"
said he, " 't is the devil of a pity that a clever
fellow like you should be a player." " Why,"
says I, in great surprise, " would you have me
a lord ?" '

' Good, good! ' says Cibber, chuckling in great
glee.

' Foote said a good thing last week to the
same noble lord,' said Garrick. ' His lordship
asked him to dine, and Foote went, daintily
decked in lace and ruffles. As they entered the
room, his lordship remarked to Foote that his
handkerchief was hanging out of his pocket.
" Thank you, my lord," said Foote, who had
purposely designed this piece of foppery, and
now resented the remark. " Thank you ; your
lordship knows the company better than I do." '

' Ah, he is a witty dog,' remarks the Woffington. ' And, as I live, here he comes.'

' Speak of the devil — ' says Quin.

<hr>

[1] Boswell's ' Johnson ' Edn. 1848, p. 556.

'And you will mention the name of one of your most intimate friends,' Foote said, entering the room, and making his bow to those assembled. ' Your servant, Mrs. Woffington.'

' A cup of tea, sir ?' said she ; and in a moment he was by her side.

'Ah, Mr. Cibber,' said he, when he was seated, ' I am glad to see you looking so well.'

' Egad, sir,' the laureate answered, 'at my age 't is well for a man if he can look at all ; ' and in the enjoyment of this apt speech, he shakes his head, until his wig in turn shakes the powder from its ponderous folds.

Presently comes a loud knocking at the door ; afterwards a heavy step is heard in the hall, and Samuel Johnson enters, bobbing his scratch-wig in friendly salutation to all assembled. Then he seats himself close by Cibber, for whom he had no love. But the poet laureate thinks well of the learned Mr. Johnson, whom by and by he will consult regarding one of the wonderful birthday odes to royalty, which are the laughing-stock of the town, but which Cibber considers it his duty to grind out annually from the heavy mill-work of his brain. In a little while the conversation turns on Macklin, whose head, Quin and Ryan avow, has been turned

by the success of his Shylock, when suddenly
up starts Foote, a merry twinkle in his eye,
as if on mischief bent. By a mere effort of
will, he rapidly changes the whole expression
of his face ; his eyebrows seem to stand like
penthouses over his eyes ; his manner assumes
an air of vast importance.

' Now, madam,' he says, turning to the Woffington, in the exact tones of Macklin, ' I,
Charles Macklin, tell you there are no good
plays among the ancients, and only one great
one among the moderns, and that is the " Merchant of Venice," and there 's only one man
can play it. Now, madam, you have been very
attentive. and I 'll tell you an anecdote of that
play. When a royal personage, who shall be
nameless, witnessed my performance of the
Jew, he sent for me to his box, and remarked,
" Sir, if I were not the prince, ha — hum —
you understand, I should wish to be Mr. Macklin." Upon which I answered, " Sir, being Mr.
Macklin, I do not desire to be — " '

At this moment a voice interrupts Foote :
' No, I 'll be damned, if I ever said that ; ' and
Macklin, who, amused by Foote's mimicry, had
stood at the door unheeded by the company
for some time, enters the room amidst the
laughter of all. Soon after, Mrs. Porter rises,

COLLEY CIBBER.

and Cibber is ready to conduct her, with great gallantry, to her chair.

' Pray, madam, do you carry firearms with you now ? ' said the old fellow, referring to an episode in her career, when she presented a pistol at the head of a highwayman who had demanded her purse whilst she drove in her chaise to Hendon.

' No, no, Mr. Cibber,' said she, laughing and shaking her head.

' Did you shoot the villain, ma'am ? ' asks the Woffington.

' No, child ; thank God, I did n't,' says she. ' For the poor fellow told me he was driven to the roads to relieve the wants of a starving family.'

' And you voluntarily gave him your purse, ma'am ? ' says Johnson, with a look of approbation.

' And, moreover,' added Cibber, ' made him an honest man by finding out the truth of his story, and raising sixty pounds for him ! '

' It was bravely done,' says the Woffington.

' But not more than you would have done, child,' she replies ; and embracing her, she departs, leaning on Colley Cibber's arm.

It is now full time for Peggy and Garrick to prepare for the theatre, so Quin and Ryan take

their leave, and Foote and Fielding depart for
the Bedford, where the former has many friends
awaiting him, with some of whom he will presently sit in the front benches of the pit at Drury
Lane, and play the part of a critic, with much
amusement to himself and to those who may
have the benefit of his remarks.

The connection between the Woffington and
Garrick did not last more than a couple of
years. Save in that art in which they both
held superior rank, they had but little in common. The Woffington was impetuous, warm-
hearted, and extravagant, whilst Garrick was
cold, cautious, and economical to a degree that
made him the butt of a thousand jests and wit-
ticisms. Boswell records that whilst Johnson
was drinking tea with them once, Garrick grum-
bled at her for making it too strong.

' Why,' said he, ' it is as red as blood.'

It was Garrick's month to pay the household
expenditure. Foote, of course, laid hold of this
trait in the great actor's character, and cracked
his jests upon it, till David waxed wrathful.
One night, when they were both leaving the
Bedford, Garrick dropped a guinea, for which
he vainly made diligent search.

' Where on earth can it have gone?' said
Foote.

'To the devil, I think,' said the other, irritably.

' Ah ! Davy,' replied the wit, ' let you alone for making a guinea go further than any one else.'

On hearing which the coffee-house gossips cackled with laughter, swore 't was prodigiously fine, and repeated it all over the town next day. Yet, for all his saving, economy was a feature which he by no means relished in his friends ; and one day, when Delane was telling Foote of Garrick's reflection on another man's parsimony, he wondered why David would not pluck the beam out of his own eye first.

' Why, so he would,' replied Foote, ' if he were sure of selling the timber.'

Notwithstanding all the disparity which existed in their characters, it seemed that, in the first glow of their friendship, Garrick had intended making this beautiful woman his wife. Macklin, who was for a time a close friend of both, and who at one period kept house with them, believed, from many conversations which he had with Peg Woffington, that she was assured Garrick would marry her. Arthur Murphy, who, as he says, enjoyed the pleasure of her acquaintance for years, heard her tell at different times that Garrick went so far as to try the wedding ring

on her finger ; whilst Boaden asserts 'it was
supposed that Garrick had really married her.'
She loved him with all the strength of her passionate nature ; hoped to spend her days by his
side ; to nestle his children at her breast ; to
share the meridian of his fame ; to cheer the
evening of his life ; but Garrick, cautious, irresolute, and mercenary, hesitated till such love as
he had ever felt for her drifted by his life.

At last the hour of their separation was at
hand.   Macklin tells us how they parted.   One
night Garrick returned to his lodgings in Bow
Street, and found the Woffington, who had not
been playing that evening, waiting up for him.
She greeted him with words that ring like music
on the toiler's ears, when coming from the lips
of a woman he loves ; but her ways were quieter
than usual, and in her eyes was a look of thought
close kin to sadness.

'Peggy,' said Garrick, sitting down beside
her in the shadow of the high, carved oak
chimney-piece, ' are you not well ? '

' I am.'

' But you seem dull.'

' I have been thinking much whilst here alone
to-night.'

' And what were the thoughts that made you
sad ? ' he asked, taking her hand in his.

'Those of my past life. David, I have been thinking of our marriage.'

'Oh, is that all?' he said, affecting to laugh lightly.

'All!' she answered; 'marriage means a great deal to a woman, — a great deal to me.'

'Yes, yes, yes,' he replied evasively, not knowing what to say, and feeling that her eyes were steadily fixed upon him.

'David,' she said quietly, but in a tone that was almost imploring, 'when is it to be?'

'What?'

'Our marriage.'

'Oh, I can't say now; we 'll talk of it another time,' he replied, rising to his feet, as if to end the conversation.

'Why not speak of it to-night?'

'Because — because I 'm tired.'

She had tact, and saw there was no use pursuing the subject then, so she let it drop.

Next morning Garrick was restless, ill at ease, and unusually silent; it was now the Woffington's turn to ask him if all was well with him.

'Well with me?' he replied, as if disturbed from a train of thought. 'Yes — that is, no;' he did not look at her as he spoke.

On the stage she exhibited vivacious audacity

and brilliant courage ; in her home she betrayed
a woman's hopes and fears.

'Will you not tell me what troubles you ? '
she said ; ' you know a burden shared loses half
its weight.'

' Well,' he said, looking down, ' I have been
thinking, Peggy, that marriage would be the
most foolish thing possible for both of us. It
would only hamper us ; the knowledge of the
fact that we were chained together would make
us miserable.'

The colour came into her face.

' And your promises ? ' she said.

' Were foolish,' he answered ; then he went
on rapidly, ' I shall always love you ; let all go
on as before — '

' Until the day comes at last when, grown
tired of me, you will cast me off as your dis-
carded mistress,' she said, rising to her feet,
whilst a light came into her eyes that he recognised as a danger-signal.

' Never, Peggy, I swear to you,' he said,
anxious to soothe her at any cost.

' Sir, you are a liar ! ' she replied, her wrath
bursting forth ; her cheeks were aflame with
humiliation, her eyes ablaze with indignation.
' You promised to make me your wife, and I
believed — and loved you ; but now that I know

DAVID GARRICK. Esq.ʳ

you as you are, I would not marry you if you were to ask me on your knees.'

' Peggy,' said he, nervously, ' don't be unreasonable. You know I love you.'

' Sir, don't insult me,' she answered, with spirit. ' To-day I leave the house, and I shall never again willingly interchange a word with you except on business.'

So saying, she quitted the room, unwilling to hear another word from him. Believing she would not put her promises into execution when her passion cooled, he left the house, to find her gone on his return in the afternoon. She had left a parcel for him containing all the presents he had given her, with a written request that he might return such as she had presented him. Now, amongst those mementoes which the liberal and warm-hearted Woffington had given him, were a handsome pair of diamond shoe-buckles of considerable value. With these he was unwilling to part, and accordingly, when he returned her presents, the most considerable of all was missing. ' She waited a month,' says Macklin, ' to see whether he would return them ; she then wrote him a letter delicately touching on the circumstance. To this, Garrick replied, saying, " as they were the only little memorials he had of the many happy hours which passed

between them, he hoped she would permit him
to keep them for her sake." Woffington saw
through this, but had too much spirit to reply ;
and he retained the buckles to the last hour of
his life.'

Garrick, according to Miss Bellamy's ' Memoirs,' ' languished for a reconciliation,' but to
this the Woffington would not consent. Soon
after her departure from Bow Street she took
up her residence at Teddington, when she sent
for her sister Polly, for whose education in a
French convent she had for years past gener-
ously paid. It was her intention to bring her
sister forward on the stage as an actress, and
in order to test her abilities she got up a private performance of ' The Distressed Mother,'
the important part of Hermione being allotted
to Miss Polly, and Andromache to a young
lady who rejoiced in the somewhat singular
names of George Anne Bellamy, of whom the
world was to hear overmuch for the next half
century. However, it was not only her names
and subsequent career which were remarkable,
but also the circumstances attending her entrance
on the world's stage.

At the age of sweet fourteen. Miss Seal, who
afterwards became the mother of George Anne
Bellamy, eloped from a highly genteel board-

ing-school in Queen's Square with my Lord Tyrawley, an Irish nobleman remarkable for his gallantry, a soldier distinguished for his bravery, a man of parts remarkable for his wit. The young lady, who was captivated by his assiduous addresses, took up her residence with my lord at Somerset House, where she was treated with all honour and respect. These two had not dwelt within one house for quite twelve months, when the noble lord was ordered to join his regiment in Ireland ; it being all the more necessary for him to depart, because his property in that country required his inspection. He therefore tore himself away from the lady whom he loved, and whom he left in a state of distraction.

Arriving in Ireland, he found his affairs in a desperate condition ; an unjust steward having taken an opportunity of enriching himself and leaving his lordship poor indeed. There was clearly but one remedy by which he could retrieve his fallen fortunes, and that was by marriage. Here were all the elements of romance, ready for the strong hand of Fate to mould into tragedy or comedy at her will. His affairs being urgent, my lord looked around him for a mate possessing wealth, and selected as the object of his choice Lady Mary Stewart, daughter of the Earl of Blessington, who had a fortune of thirty thousand pounds.

Though her ladyship was by no means handsome, her figure was described as genteel and her disposition engaging. To her, therefore, the noble lord paid his devoirs, postponing to tell the lady of his heart residing at Somerset House the necessity that had arisen for his marriage. Now it happened that my Lord Blessington had heard much of Miss Seal, who indeed called herself Lady Tyrawley; and being anxious for his daughter's happiness, he wrote a vastly polite letter to the lady, asking if her connection with her lover had been broken off, informing her at the same time that his motive for this inquiry was his lordship's approaching marriage with my Lady Mary. Whereon the lady of Somerset House fell into a most violent rage, and in her fury sent back to Earl Blessington every letter she had received from her lover, each one containing ardent protestations of eternal love and fidelity. Amongst these she, in her blind fury, enclosed one she had just received, the seal of which she had not even broken. In this Lord Tyrawley confessed all to her, his loss of fortune, the entanglement of his affairs, his approaching marriage with one whom, he said, he would tarry with not a day longer than was necessary for him to receive her portion. Then he would immediately fly on the wings of love to her who alone possessed his heart. He added by way of detail that Lady Mary was ugly and foolish, but he had elected to marry her rather than a woman who was sensible and beautiful, lest these charms might wean him from the affection of one who was his wife in the sight of Heaven. At reading this very charming and expressive letter, my Lord Blessington was flung into a state of fury bordering on madness ; when he recovered, he forbade his daughter ever to see the perfidious Tyrawley again. It is highly probable she would have obeyed, but that she had already privately married his lordship, who, not being quite certain as to the old earl's sentiments towards him, had at all hazards resolved in this manner to secure the lady, or rather her fortune. But even a guinea of this the earl now refused to give ; whereon the bridegroom demanded and obtained a separation from his wife, and, returning to England, had sufficient interest to be sent at his request as minister to one of the foreign courts.

In the next scene of this romance, Miss Seal, late of Somerset House, became an actress, and went over to Dublin, where, her connection

with Lord Tyrawley being well known, she
caused some attention.   Here she remained for
several years.   In the mean time her lover for-
gave her, frequently wrote to her, and pressed
her to join him in Lisbon.   To this she at last
consented, and arriving in that city, Lord Tyrawley, for reasons of his own, placed her in
the family of a British merchant, where he
occasionally visited her.   Whilst in Lisbon she
met with an English gentleman named Bellamy,
who, struck with her charms and unacquainted
with her situation, became enamoured of her,
and solicited her hand.   This she refused, until
one day it came to her ears that my lord had an
intrigue with a lady named Donna Anna, when,
in a fit of jealousy, she accepted Bellamy's offer,
married him, sailed with him for Ireland, and in
a few months presented him, to his infinite surprise, with a daughter.   So ungrateful was he
that he instantly abandoned her, and never saw
her again.   The child, which was named George
Anne Bellamy, being Tyrawley's offspring, his
lordship gave instructions to have her taken care
of, sent her, when of proper age, to be educated
in a French convent, and then handed her over
to the charge of a lady of quality.

In the mean time Mrs. Bellamy returned to
the stage, and as she had never exhibited any

talent in that line, she was soon reduced to extreme poverty. This condition had been considerably hastened by the fact that a mere boy whom she had recently married — the son of Sir George Walter — had stripped her of all the valuables she possessed, and dressing a companion of his in his wife's finery, set off with her to join his regiment at Gibraltar. Whilst in this state she sought an interview with her daughter, and besought her to take up her residence with her ; believing that in such case Lord Tyrawley would allow her the sum of one hundred a year, which he had stipulated to pay the lady of quality for George Anne's maintenance. Her daughter consented to the proposal, which, however, had not the result Mrs. Bellamy expected ; for not only did he refuse her an allowance, but he wrote to England renouncing his daughter forever.

At this period of her history Peg Woffington met Mrs. Bellamy, whom she had formerly known in the Dublin theatre, and with that ready generosity which was always a marked trait in her character, invited the unhappy woman and her daughter to stay at Teddington. This offer Mrs. Bellamy quickly accepted, and George Anne, being much of the same age as Miss Polly Woffington, was asked to take part

in the performance which was to test the histrionic powers of that young lady. A barn was
fitted up as a theatre for the occasion, which
was considered by Hermione and Andromache
as one of vast importance. Peg Woffington and
Mrs. Bellamy played the parts of attendants,
the great Garrick undertook the character of
Orestes, and the barn was crowded by people
of the first fashion and quality in the neighbour-
hood. It was indeed a much more eventful performance for the two young girls who sustained
the principal parts than even they imagined, for
the beautiful blue-eyed Bellamy gave such proofs
of her power as at once indicated her career,
whilst charming Polly Woffington made a conquest of the Hon. Captain Cholmondeley's
heart, and from that hour kept it through life
till death. The captain was a staid man and
good, who subsequently left the army to enter
the Church ; he was a younger son of Earl Cholmondeley, a nobleman excessively poor and
proud. Walpole, in one of his pleasant epistles,
tells us of a ' terrible disgrace ' which befell his
lordship ' t' other night at Ranelagh. You
know all the history of his letters to borrow
money to pay for damask for his fine room at
Richmond. As he was going in, in the crowd,
a woman offered him roses, — " right damask,

my lord." He concluded she had been put upon it.'

After a short courtship, Captain Cholmondeley offered his heart and hand to Miss Polly, who, having already stolen the one, now willingly enough accepted the other. When the old earl, whose household goods had by this time been seized for debt, heard of this intended alliance, he broke out in great wrath ; for not only was the object of his son's choice the sister of a player, but she had not a penny of fortune save whatever the actress in her generosity might allow her. He therefore posted off in great haste to see Peg Woffington, in order to break off the match between the young people if possible. Peg received him graciously, and by her soft words helped to turn away the first impetuous rush of his anger.

'They love each other, my lord,' she said calmly, 'and I see for both a fair prospect of happiness.'

'Love and happiness, madam ! ' said he, as if much disgusted by the probability of such a future. ' Pshaw ! let us speak sense ; the fellow has not a penny save his pay, and this marriage will be their ruin.'

' I think, my lord,' she answered, ' that honest love sometimes saves lives from wreckage.'

' But to be plain, madam,' said he, ' my son is
a man of quality, and might marry a fortune.'

' Whilst the girl he honours with his attentions is but the sister of a player,' she said.
' But, my lord, her name is spotless ; she is by
education a gentlewoman, and she shall not be
dowerless.'

At hearing this latter piece of intelligence his
lordship felt inclined to view the union with less
horror.   By degrees, indeed, he became so sub-
dued under the influence of the Woffington's
good sense and powers of fascination, that before he left he declared himself satisfied with
the marriage he had come to break off.   As he
stood up to take his departure. he begged that
dear Mrs. Woffington would forgive his being
previously offended with his son's conduct.

' Previously offended ! ' repeated she.   ' It is
I who have cause for offence, my lord.'

' Why, dear madam, how can that be ? ' asked
he, in great amazement.

' Because,' said Peggy, speaking with empha-
sis, ' I had but one beggar to support, and now
I shall have two ; ' and she curtesyed, to show
the interview was at an end.

The marriage took place in 1746, and Mrs.
Cholmondeley became ' a bright and airy ' ma-
tron, living on terms of friendship with Johnson,

Sir Joshua Reynolds, Oliver Goldsmith, and the
celebrities of her age. The Woffington lived
to see four children born to her sister, two of
whom subsequently married into the noble
houses of Townshend and Bellingham.

Now, in the same year that saw Mrs. Cholmondeley a bride, there arrived in town a young
lady, fair to look upon, who in a little while
filled that place in Garrick's life which he had
once promised Peg Woffington she should
occupy. This lady was the daughter of a respectable inhabitant of Vienna, and had been
baptised Eva Maria Veigel. Destined to become a dancer by profession, she was received
as a pupil by M. Hilferding, the celebrated
maitre de ballet, who, with others whom he
taught, introduced her to the Court, in order
to form a class for the royal children. Her
grace and beauty attracted the attention of the
Empress Maria Theresa, who desired she should
change her name from Veigel (which in Vienna
patois signifies Violet) to Violette. The admiration of the empress for the young dancer soon
becoming shared by the emperor, Frederick I.,
her imperial Majesty, in order to prevent unpleasant consequences, hurried her off to London, furnishing her at the same time with
favourable recommendations to English ladies

of the first importance, amongst whom were
the sister Countesses of Burlington and Talbot.
Both of these ladies received Mademoiselle
Violette — who, it may be remarked, arrived
in the becoming costume of a page — with open
arms, exerting, as Walpole says, · their stores of
sullen partiality and competition for her.' My
Lady Burlington had her portrait painted, and
carried her to the houses of her friends, whilst
my Lady Talbot introduced her to Frederick
Prince of Wales, the doors of whose court
were ever opened to singers, fiddlers, and
dancers.   Now, His Royal Highness was po-
litely supposed to be at once judge and patron
of all the arts, and his opinions were always
listened to, and his suggestions followed with
that attention due to a princely connoisseur.
It was an anxious moment, therefore, for the
sister countesses when he pronounced judgment
on the Violette.   To their delight, he praised
her in rapturous terms ; but in order that her
movements might acquire a greater grace, he
suggested that she should take lessons from his
favourite, Denoyer, a French gentleman of rare
talent, who, to his various professions of danc-
ing-master, fiddler, and spy, added the more
useful occupation of man midwife.   This advice the Violette, being no courtier, neglected to

follow, whereby she lost the favour and patronage of this remarkable prince.

With such support as that of the charming countesses, it was the easiest thing possible for her to get an engagement as dancer at the Opera House ; all the more so as it was at this time governed by a company of lords and men of quality, headed by my Lord Middlesex, who devoted their elegant leisure to diverting the town in this way, to the ruination of their fortunes. Accordingly she made her début in October, 1746 ; on which occasion George II. was induced to lend his august presence, as likewise that of his fair, fat German mistress, Madame Walmoden. The fashionable part of the town was thrown into a state of vast excitement over the first appearance of this dancer, who had brought with her the commendations of an empress. The Opera House was crowded by a most brilliant company ; and there, at the wings, was my Lady Burlington, ready to hold the Violette's pelisse whilst she was on, and wrap it round her when she came off the stage. Then, when the Violette danced, it was declared that never had there been witnessed such a union of grace and beauty. The whole house rose in its enthusiasm, and applauded again and again until the charming danseuse came forward, the bright colour dyeing her olive cheek, her dark eyes glistening with excitement, and bowed her thanks repeatedly. In the Wentworth correspondence, my Lord Strafford thought it worth mentioning that the Violette ' surprised her audience at her first appearance upon the stage ; for at her beginning to caper she showed a neat pair of black velvet breeches, with rolled stockings ; but finding they were unusual in England, she changes them the next time for a pair of white drawers.'

But if she lost the patronage of Frederick, Prince of Wales, she gained favour in the eyes of the king, who, though ancient, was amorous, and could yet leer at a pretty woman, and stutter compliments in broken English in their ears. According to a rare and curious pamphlet entitled ' The Memoirs of St. James's,' printed by H. Carpenter, in Fleet Street, about the year 1749, His Gracious Majesty conceived a most violent admiration for her, ' insomuch that, notwithstanding the pressing exigency of state affairs, he could not abstain so much as one evening from viewing the delightful performances of this new charmer, whose graceful personage and active accomplishments made such warm impressions on his old heart that they entirely obliterated all the affection that he had formerly

conceived for the adorable Walmoden. So that
at one moment the countess lost all the empire
over his soul that she had maintained the possession of for ever so many years. But such
was the dexterity of His Majesty that, notwithstanding his hasty temper and choleric disposition, he found means to keep his new passion a
secret from her for some time, to prevent those
domestic feuds and strifes which he must be
certain it would occasion as soon as ever she
should perceive the least spark of that flame
which burnt so vehemently in his breast.' The
king, therefore, employed a courtier, learned in
the ways of love, to plead his cause, ' content-
ing himself with the sole pleasure of enjoying
a sight of his charmer through his perspective
glass whenever she made her appearance in
public ; neither could the penetrating Walmoden
take the least umbrage at his constant attend-
ance at the opera, as she had always been a
great promoter of that amusement.'

The Violette, however, would not listen to
the pleadings of love made by the courtier on
behalf of his king. Had it, she answered, been
her desire to acquire wealth or rank at the expense of her reputation, it would have been in
her power to have accepted of such long since.
This was language foreign indeed to His Gra-

cious Majesty's ears, and his disappointment was great. To make matters worse, the Walmoden came to hear of the king's inconstancy, when in a violent rage 'she flew to the king's apartments, and meeting with him alone, upbraided him in the most bitter and opprobrious terms with his injurious treatment of her. He, no longer able to disguise the want of his former affection for her, much provoked at her coming to the knowledge of the affair, and more vexed at the lingering disappointments that had all along attended the course of his amour, was so incensed that, having no longer command over himself or his passion, nor any regard to her person or sex, he returned her volleys of upbraidings with such smart blows as soon forced her to quit the chamber.'

The Violette was, however, carefully guarded by her patronesses, and for a while all went well at the Opera House ; but she was soon destined to meet with some unpleasantness. Her refusal to take dancing lessons from Denoyer at the prince's special request was the means of bringing her into disgrace with that illustrious personage and his butterfly court ; and my Lord Middlesex, seeing in her a rival to his mistress, the famous Nardi, quarrelled with the 'most admired dancer in the world,' seized this opportunity of involving the whole *ménage* of the opera in the altercation, dissolved the committee of noble lords and pretty gentlemen, and shut up the Opera House. Great was the sensation which followed ; for my lord not only closed the Opera House, but his exchequer likewise, and declined to pay anybody, save indeed the composer Glück, who had highly diverted the town during the season by playing on a set of drinking-glasses modulated with water. In reward for this ingenious talent Glück received a bad note from his lordship, whilst the principal man dancer was, by reason of his being left penniless, arrested for debt, when the poor, fantastic fellow was mercilessly thrown into durance vile.

But the Violette was not long without another engagement, and she accordingly made her appearance at Drury Lane on the 3d of December, 1746, when she danced between the acts in company with Signor Salomon. Now the Violette had, some months before this, sat one night in the Countess of Burlington's box, and seen Garrick act, whereon she fell in love with him. When, a little later, the actor met her at one of the drawing-rooms of his fashionable friends, he had at first sight returned her love ; and from that hour Peg Woffington was forgotten. To

woo the Violette was not, however, an easy
matter, for my Lady Burlington was not pleased
to regard him in the light of a suitor with favourable eyes. Garrick had not then reached the
meridian of his fame, and the countess was of
opinion that other suitors more eligible with regard to fortune and position might claim the
hand of her beautiful protégée. There were
indeed many men of the first rank and fashion
ever ready to flutter around her wherever she
went, and amongst these was William, fifth Earl
of Coventry, whose admiration was plain to all,
though his intentions were not quite so certain
to the world. Horace Walpole tells an amusing
story of my lord following the Violette, who was
under my Lady Burlington's arm at a fine mas-
querade. Seeing this, the countess pulled off
her glove, and moved her wedding-ring up and
down her finger. 'Which,' says Walpole, 'it
seems was to signify that no other terms would
be accepted.'

A short time after, the same writer speaks of
the Violette and Garrick being at ' the prettiest
entertainment in the world,' given by the
Duchess of Richmond, which was honoured by
the presence of the King, the Princess Emily,
the Duke of Cumberland, and his mistress,
Peggy Banks. Two black princes, the Duke

of Modena, the mad Duchess of Queensbury
(dressed in a white apron and white hood),
Lady Lincoln, Lord Holderness, ' all the Fitzes
upon earth,' and everybody of fashion in town
were likewise present. The gardens at Richmond House, Whitehall, sloped down to the
Thames, on which lighters were moored. On
these ' a concert of water music was performed,'
after which a vast number of rockets were thrown
into the air ; then wheels, ranged along the rails
of the terrace, were let off, and fire-works discharged from the boats which covered the river ;
and finally there was the illumination of a pa-
vilion on the top of the slope, in the bright glare
of which the shore and the adjacent houses were
seen thronged with spectators. The King and
the Princess Emily ' bestowed themselves upon
the mob,' whilst the Duke of Cumberland, with
Peggy Banks and pretty Mrs. Pitt, who was
likewise supposed to share a corner of his
royally capacious heart, sang ' God Save the
King,' by way of setting a good example to the
crowd. The observed of all observers was
the Duke of Modena, a charming creature, who,
' instead of wearing his wig down to his nose,
to hide the humour in his face, has taken to
paint his forehead white, which, however, with
the large quantity of red that he always wears

on the rest of his face, makes him ridiculous
enough.'   The Duchess of Richmond had asked
Garrick, whilst Lady Burlington had brought
the Violette ; but the countess kept such a guard
upon her protégée that the lovers could do no
more than sigh and ogle each other the whole
night.   Presently Sabbatini, one of the Duke of
Modena's court, came up to Walpole, and asked
who all the people were.

' And who is that ? ' said he.

' C'est miladi Hartingdon, la belle fille du Duc
de Devonshire.'

' Et qui est cette autre dame ? '

It was a distressing question ; after a little
hesitation, Walpole replied, ' Mais c'est Mademoiselle Violette.'

' Et comment Mademoiselle Violette !   J'ai
connu une Mademoiselle Violette par exemple.'

Walpole begged him to look at Miss Bishop,
a fashionable beauty.

But love, who laughs at locksmiths, no doubt
behaves in the same impertinent manner to
countesses ; at all events, Garrick found opportunities of meeting the Violette in secret, when
they exchanged vows of eternal fidelity.   Long
years afterwards she used to tell how the great
actor once dressed himself up as an old woman
in order to convey her a letter.   Unable to

MRS. PITT AS LADY WISHFORT.

extinguish the love which had taken possession of the dancer's heart for Garrick, my Lady Burlington at last gave her consent to their union, and one fine morning early in June, 1749, the dancer and the actor were wedded. A marriage settlement of ten thousand pounds was made upon the bride ; my Lady Burlington giving six thousand, and Garrick the remaining sum.

It happened that in 1747, a period at which Garrick had begun to give proof of his devotion to the Violette, he became joint patentee with Lacy, of Drury Lane Theatre, a circumstance especially disagreeable to the Woffington, whose engagement to Lacy obliged her to continue a member of his company for the coming season. Garrick, according to Macklin, felt likewise embarrassed ; but what made the Woffington's ' situation more critical,' he adds, ' was the interference of Mrs. Cibber, Pritchard, and Clive, particularly the latter, who, being naturally quick as well as coarse in her passion, frequently drew upon her the sarcastic replies of Woffington, who made battle with a better grace and the utmost composure of temper.'

The first hour she was free, she therefore withdrew her services from Drury Lane, and went over to Covent Garden, under Rich's management, and during the first months of her

engagement here won a fresh triumph by her
personation of Lady Jane Grey in Rowe's tragedy
of that name.   Never, indeed, it was said, was
her beautiful face, her graceful figure, seen to
better advantage, whilst her pathos moved the
house to tears.   Not satisfied with the success
she had already gained, she, whilst the theatre
was closed during the summer months of 1748,
crossed over to Paris, in order to take lessons
from the famous Mademoiselle Dumesnil.   From
the day when little Peg Woffington had learned
French and dancing from Madame Violante,
she had never failed to seize on every possible
opportunity of improving herself ; and now, not
satisfied with her position as the first actress in
England, she, recognising the greater excellence
of the Frenchwoman, resolved to become her
pupil.   The Dumesnil was at this time at the
head of her profession in France.   Her elocution
was considered unsurpassed, her actions pronounced classical in their grace, and her manner
the reflection of Nature, it being her chief
study to identify herself with the character she
personated.   Peg Woffington studied her closely,
and, on her return from Paris, played Veturia,
in Thomson's ' Coriolanus,' which the town
vastly admired.   Like a true artist, it was the
ambition of her life to gain the public favour,

and the result was that which usually attends
such endeavours. In Veturia she sacrificed her
beauty to the propriety of the character by painting her face with wrinkles and other unlovely
signs of age ; and again she frequently accepted
inferior parts in plays in order to strengthen the
cast. Tate Wilkinson bears evidence that ' she
never permitted her love of pleasure and con-
viviality to occasion the least defect in her duty
to the public as a performer. Six nights in the
week has been often her appointed lot for playing, without murmuring ; she was ever ready at
the call of the audience, and though in possession of all the first line of characters, yet she
never thought it improper or a degradation of
her consequence to constantly play parts which
are mentioned as insults in the country if offered
to a lady of consequence.

So much could not be said for other actresses of her time, who delighted in harassing
the souls of their managers by the refusal of
parts, as well as by convenient illnesses which
were wont to attack them at their own sweet
wills. This was, indeed, a constant practice
not only with Mrs. Cibber, but with Quin and
Barry likewise, who were at this time members
of the Covent Garden company. At a few
hours' notice they frequently sent word that

they were attacked with an illness, whereon
the tragedies they were advertised to perform
were substituted for the sprightly comedies in
which Peg Woffington was always certain to
draw a crowded house. Considering this treatment unjust, the latter protested against it ; but
this not having the desired effect, she threatened that if it occurred again, she would likewise be seized by a convenient illness. Soon
after it happened that Mrs. Cibber was announced to play Jane Shore, but almost at
the last moment she declared herself too indisposed to act, and Peg Woffington was instead
announced to perform Sir Harry Wildair ; but
just as the doors of the playhouse were opened,
she despatched a message to the manager that
she also had suddenly been taken ill, and would
be unable to play that evening. Therefore the
only thing which could be done was to substi-
tute another comedy. This the remaining members of the company performed so badly that
the audience became incensed to a degree, and
resolved to punish the offending absentees in
general for their capricious conduct, and Peg
Woffington in particular for having disappointed them on this special occasion.   Accordingly, when, a couple of nights later, she
appeared as Lady Jane Grey, for the first time

in her life she was received with a storm of dis-
approbation. She stood still a moment speech-
less from surprise, when the audience bade her
ask pardon.

‘ Whoever saw her that night,’ says Tate Wilkinson, who tells the story in his interesting
memoirs, ‘ will own they never beheld any figure half so beautiful since. Her anger gave a
glow to her complexion, and even added lustre
to her charming eyes. She behaved with great
resolution, and treated their rudeness with glorious contempt. She left the stage, was called
for, and with infinite persuasion was prevailed
upon to return. She did return, walked forward, and told them she was then ready and
willing to perform her character if they chose
to permit her ; that the decision was theirs, *on*
or *off*, just as they pleased, — it was a matter of
indifference to her. The *ons* had it, and all
went smoothly afterwards.’

She, however, attributed the origin of the
storm to the contrivance of the manager, who
took this means of frightening her against being
ill at an inopportune moment. She therefore
resented it as an insult, and refused to engage
herself to him at the end of the season. The
only other theatre opened to her in London
was Drury Lane, and Garrick being manager

of this, she was reluctant to serve under his generalship. At this crisis she turned her thoughts to the playhouses of her native city, crossed the Channel, and was engaged by Tom Sheridan, father of the famous dramatist, for the season of 1751, at a salary of four hundred pounds.

MR. SHERIDAN AS CATO.

CHAPTER IX.

Thomas Sheridan, the Manager. — Letter to Garrick. — Becomes a Manager. — Conditions of the Playhouse. — A Theatrical Riot and its Result. — Dublin before the Union. — Lionel, Duke of Dorset, at the Castle. — Diversions of the Town. — High Life and Low. — Mrs. Butler, Miss Bellamy, and David Garrick. — A Strange Love-letter. — Mrs. Butler's Present.

THOMAS SHERIDAN, the manager of the Dublin theatres, with whom Peg Woffington now engaged, was a man whose name is intimately connected with the history of the Irish stage. He was son of the Rev. Dr. Sheridan and godson of poor Dean Swift of witty memory. He had been educated at Westminster School, and had graduated at Trinity College, Dublin, where he was yet reading for a fellowship when David Garrick paid his first visit to the Irish capital. Seeing the great actor perform, Sheridan was seized by stage fever, and, abandoning all idea of becoming a fellow, he, to the intense disgust and indignation of his friends, left college and became a player. His appearance on the boards of Smock Alley Thea-

tre on the 29th of January, 1743, in the character of Richard III., caused considerable
sensation in the town.   He was in the twenty-
third year of his age ; his appearance was
handsome, his voice mellow and expressive,
and his *début* was a decided success.   He next
played Othello, Hamlet, Cato, and Brutus, and
his acting gained so rapidly on the town that he
became the rage ; his name was on all men s lips.
' So great,' says Davis, ' was his influence over
the Dublin audience, that Quin, who arrived in
that city during the first warm glow of Mr.
Sheridan's prosperity, with an intention to act
a number of characters, and put a handsome
sum of money in his pocket (a custom which
he had often practised), was obliged to quit the
metropolis with disgust, if not in disgrace.   He
was told by the proprietors that all the acting
days during the remainder of the winter were
engaged to the new actor.'

His fame rapidly spread across the Channel,
and Garrick wrote to him suggesting that he
might share the honours of London town with
him.   Sheridan's interesting reply to this is
preserved in the Garrick correspondence, dated
April, 1743.   He commences by apologizing
for not having answered Garrick's obliging letter with greater speed, more than a fortnight

having passed since he had received it ; but
during that time he had had three new characters to study as well as to play, — Othello being
one of them. He thanks him for his invitation
to pass the summer with him at Walton, — an
enjoyment which the posture of his affairs will
not permit. However, it is not improbable but
that he may see London about the middle of
May, as he intends to take a jaunt of pleasure
there if all goes well. Then he continues : ' I
have not as yet fixed any scheme for the next
winter, but I have been offered such advan-
tageous terms as will, I believe, detain me here
till January at least. As to your proposal of
our playing together, I am afraid I have too
many powerful reasons against it : a well-cut
pebble may pass for a diamond till a fine brilliant is placed near it and puts it out of coun-
tenance. (A bold metaphor that ; or, as Bayes
says, " Egad, that 's one of my bold strokes ! ")
Besides, we should clash so much in regard to
characters that I am afraid it is impossible we
can be in the same house. Richard, Hamlet,
and Lear, as they are your favourite characters,
are mine also ; and though you were so condescending to say I might appear in any part of
yours, yet I question whether the town would
bear to see a worse performer in one of your

characters in the same house with you, though
they might endure him in another.' He has,
however, a scheme to propose to Garrick, which
at first view may seem a little extraordinary, but
which, if rightly considered, might turn to the
advantage of both; which is, that Garrick might
be brought to divide his immortality with him,
when, like Castor and Pollux, they might always
appear in different hemispheres, or, in plain
English, they might divide the kingdoms between them, one playing one winter in Dublin
and another in London, — when they would be
always new in both kingdoms, and consequently
the more followed. 'But more of this,' he
concludes, ' when I have the pleasure of meeting you. Pray remember my best respects to
Mrs. Woffington. I should own myself unpar-
donable in not having wrote to her, were it in
my power ; but I have been already sufficiently
punished at the loss of so agreeable a correspondent, for I assure you I have a long time
envied her pretty Chronon that pleasure ; as
soon as I have a moment to spare, I intend to
do myself the honour to write to her.'

Sheridan in a short time quarrelled with the
manager of Smock Alley, when he went over to
the opposition playhouse in Aungier Street, and
back again to the theatre in which he made his

first appearance. Dissatisfied with the condition of things here, he crossed the Channel, and in March, 1744, played at Covent Garden in opposition to Garrick, to which theatre he succeeded in drawing great audiences. But two playhouses in Dublin could not find sufficient support ; the proprietors, therefore, for once in a way acted wisely in agreeing that the one company should play alternately at each house, and moreover invited Sheridan to return and take the full management. This he accepted, and came back to Dublin within the same year as he had quitted it.

Now, at this period the Dublin theatres had been fast hastening to ruin from bad management, the wretched acting of stock companies, and certain liberties allowed a portion of the audiences. Amongst the latter it was the habit of the undergraduates from the college to visit the theatre for the mid-day rehearsal, crowding the stage to such an extent that the players were surrounded by a circle of those precocious youths, who made audible comments not always of the most complimentary order, and cracked jests of the freest character. At night these 'college boys,' as they were called, together with the young men of quality about town, thronged behind the scenes or crowded the

green-room, where they diverted themselves according to their desires, — flocking on to the
stage when the curtain went up, where they
lounged at the entrances, crossed before the
footlights, and exchanged civilities or the reverse with the pit and boxes at their own sweet
wills during the performance. These abuses
Sheridan was determined to abolish ; but time-
honoured customs that admitted such pleasant
liberties were not to be removed in a day, and
for three years he struggled against them with
but slight success. At last a circumstance occurred which, though at first fraught with dis-
cord and danger, resulted in gaining him the
assistance of the town in preserving order and
decency in his theatre.

It happened one night in January, 1747, whilst
the comedy of 'Æsop' was being performed,
a young man of quality named Kelly entered
the theatre. This pretty fellow was much in-
flamed with wine, and was therefore in a mood
to divert himself ; for which laudable purpose
he presently climbed over the spikes, with which
it was at that time found necessary to divide the
orchestra from the pit. Getting on to the stage
in this manner, he rushed into the green-room,
where he met Mrs. Dyer, an actress of excellent character, whom he addressed in terms that

obliged her and the other women present to fly
to their respective dressing-rooms, to which he
promptly followed them.   Hearing the noise,
Sheridan, who was in his private room, came
out, and seeing Kelly was more merry than
wise, ordered some of his men to carry him
to the pit from whence he came.   At this interference with his pleasure the pretty young
gentleman was mighty indignant, and, taking
a basket from one of the orange-women who
were then allowed to vend fruit in the pit, he,
when Sheridan appeared, commenced to pelt
him with oranges.   So excellent was his aim,
that one of them struck the visor the manager
wore in his character of Æsop, and cut his
forehead ;   on this, Sheridan appealed to the
audience.   Kelly then stood up and informed
him he was a scoundrel and a rascal, to which
the manager replied he was as good a gentleman
as he ; those in the pit then obliged Kelly to sit
down.   But at the end of the play his spirit
was up again ; and, bent on mischief, he forced
his way through the stage door, rushed to Sheridan's room, and told him he was a rascal and a
scoundrel.   By way of rewarding him for such
information, the manager thrashed him soundly,
and had him turned out of doors.   With face
sadly swollen and blood-smeared, and clothes

torn and soiled, this young gentleman, alas ! no
longer pretty, betook himself to the Brown
Bear Coffee House, where those of his kind
most did congregate. To them he told a lamentable tale, garnished with such additions
and improvements as were best calculated to
rouse the ire sleeping in their ruffle-adorned
breasts. Sheridan, quoth he, had said he was
as good a gentleman as any in the house ; and
when he (Kelly), burning with exasperation,
had gone behind the scenes to avenge this insult, he had been held hand and foot by the
manager's servants, whilst the said manager beat
him. Then, said they, this shall not be. No
scoundrel play-actor shall be allowed to beat
a pretty gentleman with impunity. If such
were permitted, why, the end of the world
might be expected any day. Therefore, great
was their indignation, and fervent their vows of
vengeance, which not only threatened Sheridan,
but those who should take his part. A theatrical storm was therefore promptly expected. A
few days later, Sheridan was advertised to play
Horatio in ' The Fair Penitent,' upon which he
received several letters, cards, and messages
from his friends, begging him not to venture
outside his door that evening, and to have his
house well guarded.

This advice he complied with, fortunately for himself, for the theatre was that night packed with Kelly's friends. When it was announced that Sheridan was unable to appear, about fifty of those, with Kelly at their head, rose in the pit, and with a cry of rage and disappointment scrambled on to the stage ; from thence they immediately rushed to the green-room and the dressing-rooms, forcing open all doors that were locked, in eager pursuit of their prey. But the manager was not to be found. They next proceeded to the wardrobe, and, by way of feeling if he were in any of the chests or presses, they ran their swords through the valuable costumes these contained. They next set out for his house in Dorset Street ; but seeing it was guarded, and believing safety the better part of valour, they retired, harbouring their vengeance for another occasion. Next day nothing was spoken of all over Dublin but this attempted outrage. The citizens had always a keen interest in matters theatrical, and this subject of the hour was regarded by one and all almost as a matter of personal interest. The town was therefore divided into two parties, unequal in number, it must be confessed, the majority being in favour of Sheridan. For a month the theatre was closed, during which

period letters relative to the quarrel were published almost daily in the ' Dublin Journal,'
whilst pamphlets teemed from the press. The
decorum of the stage and the defence of morality were at stake, one party asserted ; whilst the
other complained of the infringement of time-
honoured rights, and the insult given to a man
of quality. The riot grew more bitter daily,
and spread from the city all over the kingdom.

At the end of the fourth week the greater
part of the town declared it would no longer be
deprived of its usual and favourite amusement.
Sheridan was therefore requested to open the
theatre, when he was assured he would receive powerful protection. He accordingly in
a short time announced the performance of
Richard III., his favourite character. No
sooner were the doors of the theatre opened,
than the house was filled by Sheridan's friends,
to the vast surprise of the rioters, who arrived
late and in comparatively small numbers. They,
however, considered themselves sufficient to create a disturbance ; and when Sheridan appeared,
they set up a cry of ' Submission, submission,
submission ! off, off, off ! ' which was answered
by a counter-cry of ' No submission ! on with
the play ! ' At this, a citizen of fair renown,
named Charles Lucas, stood up in the pit and

claimed a hearing. Every person in the house, he said, came to receive the entertainment promised in the bill, for which he paid his money. The actors were therefore the servants of the audience, and under their protection during the performance ; and he was of opinion that every insult or interruption given them in the discharge of their duty was offered to the public. In conclusion, he would ask those who were in favour of the decency and freedom of the stage to hold up their hands ; from which sign it might be learned if the play was to proceed or not. Amidst shouts of applause, more than two thirds of those present held up their hands ; at which the rioters left the house, and the play ended peacefully. But the Kellyites were not yet suppressed ; their threats of vengeance continued ; they were determined to ruin the manager. By way of indicating the spirit which animated them, they set upon Charles Lucas two nights after his speech, and beat him severely whilst he was peaceably walking through Sackville Street. Next day he had an advertisement printed and distributed all over the town, offering a reward of five pounds for the arrest of a number of disorderly persons in the garb of gentlemen, who had assaulted him in a cowardly manner.

Sheridan, seeing the rioters were yet bent

upon injuring him, closed the theatre again, and
it was not for some weeks later that he once
more ventured to open it, when 'The Fair
Penitent' was announced to be performed for
the benefit of the Hospital for Incurables. The
governors of this institute, who were all persons
of consequence, assured the manager they would
take it on themselves to defend him from danger
or insult, and several ladies of quality promised
their presence on the occasion. When the night
came, a brilliant house assembled; the governors
of the hospital were all present, carrying white
wands; ladies of the first fashion filled the boxes,
and over a hundred of them had to be accommodated with seats on the stage. It was, however,
noticed, that about thirty young men had taken
possession of the middle part of the first three
benches in the pit. When the curtain rose,
Sheridan was in due state ushered on the stage
by some of the governors, when he came forward to speak a prologue. No sooner, however, had he appeared, than the thirty men in
front, who, it was now seen, were all armed,
rose up in a body and authoritatively ordered
him off. The manager bowed to the house and
withdrew, when a violent argument between
these men and the governors ensued. Amongst
the latter was a student from the college in his

bachelor's gown, who spoke with great warmth
in Sheridan's defence, in return for which one
of the rioters struck him with an apple and
called him a scoundrel. At this insult offered to
one of their body, several of the undergraduates
who were present flew like feathered Mercury
to the college, and in a short time returned with
a number of their fellow-students, all armed.
Meanwhile the rioters, seeing the 'college boys'
had rushed from the house, guessed their errand
and quickly left the pit. The undergraduates
were therefore disappointed of their prey, but
their blood being up, they were not easily paci-
fied. They had during this disturbance remained
neutral, but now they were glad to take this
opportunity of one of their body being insulted
to espouse the cause of a man who had left old
Trinity to become a player. They had therefore a double incentive in punishing the rioters.
Not finding them at the theatre, they searched
every club, coffee-house, and tavern in the town,
but in vain. They then returned to the college,
baffled for the present, but more determined on
vengeance than ever, and held a council of war
which lasted all night. Next morning, when
the gates were opened, out they flocked to a
man, armed and ready for combat. and sepa-
rating into various bodies, went in search of the

rioters at their divers residences. They were informed that the man who had fired the apple had but just come up from the country; but not being aware of his abode, they were compelled to inquire at lodging-houses and hotels for him, and it was not until eleven o'clock that he was led a captive inside the college gates. The city was meanwhile in a tumult of excitement; the guardians of the peace seldom interfered with the students; the shop-keepers, fearing a general riot, had not opened their doors; business was suspended, and many of the rioters, conscious of the search which was being made for them, rushed in fear of their lives to the Court of Chancery, where the Chancellor was sitting, and besought his protection.

Having secured the principal offender, a great number of the undergraduates next sallied forth to look for a young officer, a gay jack-a-dandy, who had likewise made himself specially offensive. It was known that he lived in his father's house in Capel Street, which was found by the students barricaded and guarded. These obstacles but made them more desperate, and afforded them a pleasant though dangerous incentive to their efforts. A raid was promptly made, a skilful breach effected, the offender seized, placed in a hackney-coach, and, amidst loud huzzas, hurried within the walls of Trinity. Then came the punishments. The first offender was compelled to travel on his bare knees round all the courts of the college, and to repeat a form of humble apology prepared the previous night ; the second offender was, by reason of his holding the king's commission, allowed to read the apology standing. Both were glad to escape with a chastisement which, if humiliating, at least mercifully left them whole bones.

The theatre was now ordered by the Lords Justices to be closed, and the next scene of this eventful drama was laid in court, — Sheridan having taken an action against Kelly for assault, and damages done to the theatrical wardrobe ; the manager in return being indicted for assault and battery. Sheridan was tried first ; but so clearly and satisfactorily was it proved he had been incited to a breach of the peace that the jury, without leaving their box, acquitted him. Then came Kelly's turn. The first witness called was the prosecutor. The chief counsel for the defence rose up with that air of dignity becoming one learned in the law, and said he vastly desired to see a curiosity. He had seen a gentleman soldier, likewise a gentleman tailor (laughter in court), but he had never yet seen a gentleman actor (great laughter). On which Sheridan turned to him calmly, and said, ' Sir, you see one now,' — an answer which was received with such prodigious applause that it dawned on the learned gentleman he had made a mistake. Justice Ward tried the case, which ended by Kelly being sentenced to three months' imprisonment and fined five hundred pounds. This undreamt of result fell like a thunderbolt on Kelly. At the commencement of the suit it was rumoured that a subscription would be made to defray his law expenses ; but in the hour of trial his friends deserted him, and left him to meet his fate alone. A week's imprisonment seemed to have the wholesome effect of bringing him to his senses, for at the expiration of that period he, with words of sorrow and humility, applied to Sheridan that he might petition the court in favour of lightening his sentence, which this man, whom he had called a scoundrel, accordingly did, with such good effect that the fine was remitted, and Sheridan further pledging himself as bail for the prisoner's future good conduct, that young gentleman was restored to liberty once more.

Dublin in the days before the Union was the gay capital of a prosperous nation, and boasted of a society at once cultured, fashionable, and brilliant. A native parliament sat in College Green ; Irish peers and commons of note dwelt in the city ; and the lord lieutenant, then surrounded by regal pomp and circumstances of state, held court at the Castle. Irish society, smaller in its circle than that which revolved round the Court of St. James's, was not less brilliant ; the beauty of its women was proverbial, the sprightliness of its men characteristic. By nature a pleasure-loving people, their days and nights were chiefly devoted to the pursuit of amusement ; and the diaries and memoirs of those who formed part of the gay and goodly crowd that held revelry in the middle of the last century in the Irish capital, present us with a series of vivacious and interesting pictures.

The chief and most fashionable promenade in the city was St. Stephen's Green, which was to the residents of the Irish capital what the Mall was to Londoners. Situated in the centre of the town, it was planted with trees, and boasted broad and shady walks, where ladies of quality and men of fashion disported themselves in the mornings. Having taken the air here, they visited and went to dinner betimes. Then in fair weather they drove in great coaches or rode on horseback to the Phœnix Park, — a piece of ground which, with its delightful wood and

turfy ground, rivalled St. James's or Hyde
Park. Moreover, it commanded an agreeable
prospect of the Dublin Mountains, from which
healthful breezes blew. In the midst of the
wood, in view of the column surmounted by
the fabulous bird which gives its name to the
park, the gift of Lord Chesterfield, a circular-
shaped space was cleared, where society met
and talked of routs and *ridotti*, plays and concerts, its neighbours' shortcomings, and all the
delightful scandal of the town.

The polite Lord Chesterfield, just mentioned,
during his reign as lord lieutenant, a few years
before the Woffington's second visit to her native city, had left behind him reminiscences of
costly splendour that equalled, if not eclipsed,
the glory of St James's. He had added to the
Castle a new room, which was allowed to be
the most magnificent in the three kingdoms.
In this he held balls, to which the nobility of
the land were bidden, where, when dancing
was over, says Victor, quaintly enough, ' the
company retired to an apartment, to a cold supper, with all kinds of the best wines and sweetmeats. The whole apartment was most elegantly
disposed and ornamented with transparent paintings, through which was cast a shade like moon-
light, flutes and other soft instruments playing

SARAH JENNINGS, DUCHESS OF MARLBOROUGH.

all the while, but, like the candles, unseen. At each end of the building, through which the company passed, were placed fountains of lavender water that diffused a most grateful odour through this fairy scene, which surpassed everything of the kind in Spenser, as it proved not only a fine feast for the imagination, but after the dream, for our sensualities by the excellent substantials at the sideboard.'

The luxurious earl had been succeeded for a brief while by my Lord Harrington, who in turn gave place to Lionel, Duke of Dorset. — his grace arriving in Ireland towards the autumn of 1751, in the same month as Peg Woffington made her appearance at Smock Alley playhouse. The sharp-tongued Sarah, Duchess of Marlborough, who seldom indeed had a good word to say of any one, writes in a charmingly characteristic manner of his grace. 'Such a wretch as he is I hardly know,' says the eccentric duchess; 'and his wife, whose passion is only for money, assists him in his odious affair with Lady Betty Jermyn, who has a great deal to dispose of.' Wretch or no wretch, he was for a time at least popular in the Irish capital; and exceeding great was the throng of courtiers that flocked to the Castle drawing-rooms during his reign. Mrs. Delany, in one of her letters, pleasantly gossips

of going to the Vice-regal Court one birthday
in her coach, whilst a friend of hers, whom she
styles Madame, went thither in her sedan ' with
her three footmen in Saxon green, with orange-
coloured cockades,' marching in step before
her. ' Can you tell why she desired me to go
with her?' asks Mrs. Delany, giving way to a
bit of feminine pique. ' I can. She was su-
perb in brown and gold and diamonds ; I was
clad in purple and white silk I bought when
last year in England, and my littleness set off
her greatness.' After half an hour's stoppage
on the way, caused by the vast number of
coaches and chairs blocking the thoroughfares
leading courtwards, this blaze of colour reached
the Castle and took its way to the drawing-
room, where the duke and duchess came, ' half
an hour after one, very graceful and princely.
The duchess had a blue paduasoy, embroidered
very richly with gold, and there was a great
deal of handsome finery.' Presently a band
and choir, under the direction of Dubourg, gave
a birthday song in honour of royalty, which was
vastly admired ; and in the evening a ball was
held in the old beef-eaters' hall. — an apartment
capable of holding seven hundred persons.

  The crowd assembled on this occasion was
so prodigious that the ladies were seated on an

amphitheatre at one end of the room in rows
one above another, so that the last row almost
touched the ceiling, — presenting an appearance
which reminded some of the gentlemen of ' a
Cupid's paradise in a puppet show.' In this
vast room, with its blaze of lights and shining
floor, women with narrow waists, bare breasts,
and far-extending hoops danced stately minuets
with men in powdered wigs, velvet coats, and
high-heeled shoes ; curtesying, undulating, advancing, and retreating with slow pace and a
world of grace to the measured music discoursed
by French horns. In an apartment at the end
of a suite, sat the Duchess of Dorset, playing
basset with some dowagers whose dancing days
were over, whilst in the rooms adjoining were
quadrille parties, where those who had danced
might saunter up and down and look on at the
games. Finally, the duke and duchess, who
had been vastly obliging all the evening, led the
way to supper, which was laid in the council-
chamber. ' In the midst of this apartment was
placed a holly-tree illuminated by a hundred
wax tapers ; round it was placed all sorts of
meat, fruit, and sweetmeats ; servants waited
and were encompassed round by a table, to
which the company came by turns to take what
they wanted. When the doors were first opened,

the hurly-burly is not to be described, — squalling, shrieking, all sorts of noises ; some ladies lost their lappets, others were trod upon, and poor Lady Santry almost lost her breath in the scuffle, and fanned herself two hours before she could recover herself enough to know if she was dead or alive.'

But it was not only at the Castle that great receptions were held and lively balls given. The stately and magnificent mansions of the nobility, faced with sparkling granite native to the Wicklow Hills, and adorned by the genius of foreign artists, which retain traces of their beauty to the present day, though converted into schools or let in tenements, were in those times the scenes of constant revelry. My Lord Grandison delighted in assembling the wit and beauty of the capital round a board heavy from the weight of golden candelabra and services of silver. Lord Mountjoy gave balls that were the talk of the city. His lordship was a gay man, though not a brave ; for when he quarrelled with old Norse the gambler, my lord refused to fight him, whereon the man who loved cards, by way of having revenge in a fashion truly Hibernian, went home and cut his own throat, — a fact that by no means prevented Lord Mountjoy from diverting himself as usual.

TRINITY COLLEGE, DUBLIN

Then Lady Doneraile had famous quadrille parties at her handsome mansion in Dawson Street, my Lord Strangford and his lady gave delightful concerts. and Bishop Clayton's wife, who loved this world well, opened the doors of her big mansion, with a front like Devonshire House, situated in Stephen's Green, every Wednesday for the reception of her friends, who passed through a great hall filled with servants in showy liveries. The reception-room was 'wainscoted with oak, the panels all carved, and the doors and chimney finished with a very fine high carving, the ceiling stucco, the window-curtains and chairs yellow Genoa damask, portraits and landscapes very well done round the room, marble tables between the windows, and looking-glasses with gilt frames, besides *virtu* and busts that his lordship brought from Italy, the floor being covered with the finest Persian carpet that ever was seen.'

The bishop did not love the things of earth less than his buxom spouse, and ' kept a very handsome table, six dishes of meat being constantly at dinner, and six plates at supper.' The clergy, indeed, took no ordinary share in entertaining the town, an excellent example being set them by the primate, whose choice dinners and cosy suppers were luxuries long to be remembered. This right reverend and easy-going man's vocation for the Church had been decided, not so much by divine inspiration as by a game of dice. The story is told in one of Dean Swift's letters, given in Nichol's ' Literary Illustrations.' When the Duke of Dorset, who had been lord lieutenant about sixteen years previous to his appointment to that office in 1751, was quitting Ireland, he had but two pre-ferments to bestow, — a cornetcy and a church living, value two hundred a year. For the former, two of the duke's friends, Lushington and Stone, anxiously contended, and not being able to settle the matter amicably between them, it was agreed that dice should decide which would become a pastor of souls and which a gay and gallant soldier. Lushington won the game, and entered the army, whilst Stone went into the Church. Being a very ingenious man, he quickly rose in his profession to be Bishop of Derry and subsequently Archbishop of Armagh and primate. Once when this worthy man was about to give a dinner, in honour of the birth-day of his friend and patron, the Duke of Dor-set, he ordered a Perigord pie for the occasion, with directions to have this delicacy directed to a merchant of his acquaintance. The pie ar-rived in the absence of the merchant, whose

wife, supposing it to be a present from one of
her husband's friends abroad, sent out and invited some of her neighbours to sup with her at
an early date. But on the very day when these
good people were to regale themselves, the
primate's *maître d'hôtel*, who had hitherto inquired in vain for the lost pie, hearing of the
good lady's hospitable intentions, swooped down
on her, and carried it away.

' I own,' writes Mrs. Delany, who tells the
story, ' I am sorry they did not eat it ; such ex-
pensive rarities do not become the table of a
prelate, who ought not to ape the fantastical
luxuriances of fashionable tables.' This charming correspondent likewise speaks of the dinners
of the Bishop of Elphin, whose daughter ' was
brought up like a princess.' The bishop ' lives
well,' she writes ; ' but high living is too much
the fashion here. You are not invited to dinner
to any private gentleman of a thousand a year
or less, that does not give you seven dishes at
one course, and Burgundy and Champagne ; and
these dinners they give once or twice a week.'

A taste for painting and music likewise obtained, and was highly encouraged, — for the
former, by the exhibitions at the Royal Academy
in Shaw's Court, Dame Street ; for the latter by
the performances of oratorios constantly sung at

St. Patrick's cathedral, and concerts which were always attended by vast crowds. An excellent entertainment was given every Wednesday during the season by a musical society, the members of which were all men of quality, some of whom played prodigiously well, notably Mr. Brownlow, M.P., a fine executor on the harpsichord, and Captain Reade, who performed on the German flute to great perfection. At the Philharmonic Room in Fishamble Street, concerts were almost nightly given, the place ' being illuminated with wax and the whole conducted in the genteelest manner.' Likewise at the Great Music Room in Crow Street there was a weekly concert given, 'the instrumental parts by Messrs. Marella, Lee, Storace, De Boeck, and others ; the vocal by Mr. Sullivan. To begin exactly at seven o'clock and continue until nine each night, after which there will be a *ridotto*, with tea, coffee, chocolate, jellies, cards, and all sorts of liquids of the best kind at the usual prices, and suppers by giving notice the day before.'

By way of adding to the diversion of the town, subscription balls were got up by the beaux, headed by Lord Belfreld, and were occasionally held in one of the theatres, converted for the time being into a ball-room. One of these, which was given whilst the Woffington was

in Dublin, cost seven hundred pounds. The
theatre in which it took place was dressed to
represent a wood, space being left in the middle
for thirty couples to dance. At one end was a
portico of Doric pillars, lighted by green wax
candles, arranged in baskets of flowers ; then
there was a Gothic temple in which refreshments
were served, and a jasmine bower where lovers
whispered, and a grotto with rustic arches,
where the musicians, dressed as shepherds and
shepherdesses, discoursed sweet sounds. The
trees which lined the walls were the veritable
growth of Nature, adorned by art in the shape
of cotton leaves. The Duke and Duchess of
Dorset were present, as were all the members
of the polite world which the city numbered,
and enjoyed themselves vastly, dancing being
kept up long after daylight did appear. One of
the most inveterate dancers of the night was a
certain Captain Folliat, ' a man of six feet odd
inches high, black, awkward, roaring, ramping.'
His gaunt figure was seen continually in every
dance. ' I thought,' says a partner of his whom
he most affected on this occasion, ' he would
have shook my arms off, and crushed my toes to
atoms ; every moment he did some blundering
thing, and as often asked " my ladyship's pardon." I was pitied by the whole company ; at

I. — 16

last I resolved to dispatch him with dancing,
since he was not worth my conquest any other
way. I called a council about it, having some
scruples of conscience, and fearing he might
appear and haunt me after his death staggered
my resolutions ; but when it was made plain to
me that I should do the world a great piece of
service by dispatching him, it solved all my
scruples, and I had no more qualms about it.
In the midst of his furious dancing, when he was
throwing his arms about him most outrageously
(just like a card scaramouch on a stick), snap
went something that we all thought had been
the main bone of his leg ; but it proved only a
bone of his toe. Notwithstanding this he fought
upon his stumps, and would not spare me one
dance.'

Besides these social amusements, there were
great reviews held frequently in the park, where
the troops, to quote from the ' Dublin Journal,'
' went through their different evolutions and
firings with the greatest exactness, to the satisfaction of the duke and the general officers.'
These reviews were attended by all the fashionable world, Her Grace of Dorset at its head in
a yellow coach and six horses, very fine to see.
Then the citizens frequented the public gardens
every night, they being open to all ; where,

says Benjamin Victor, in writing to the Countess
of Orrery, ' great regularity and decency is un-
accountably preserved, and of course unusual
dulness is the consequence. If no valiant captain will knock down a lady, nor any lady cock
her pistol at her perfidious man (both these
shocking events happened lately in the public
gardens), we must remain in this stupid state of
tranquillity.' At Marlborough Green there were
bi-weekly entertainments made up of dancing,
fiddling, and singing by Miss Rachel Baptist, —
an African lady, who wore a wreath of roses
and clad her sable person in orange silk. So
multiform, indeed, were its attractions, that the
green was usually attended by vast crowds.

So far as cleanliness morally and physically
went, Dublin was much in the same condition as
the sister capital. An advertisement in ' Faulkner's Journal,' October 2, 1751, informs the
inhabitants of the city ' they are requested by
the Lord Mayor to sweep the dirt before their
houses twice every week into the Channel, for
the speedier removal of the same by the scav-
engers, otherwise they will be fined.' The same
journal says, ' Street and house robberies are
now become so common in this city that it is
dangerous to be out late on evenings; and hats,
capuchins, books, etc., are frequently stolen

from churches and other places of worship in
the time of divine service.' This statement is
verified by the oftentimes quaint reports in the
daily papers, a few of which will serve to illus-
trate the general condition of the town. ' Last
Thursday,' says ' Faulkner's Journal,' October
15, 1751, ' a young gentleman was attacked by
a single highwayman near Harold's Cross, who
robbed him of his gold watch, twenty guineas,
three crowns, and a shilling. He rode a bay
gelding about fourteen hands and a half high,
was dressed in a white fustian frock, a scarlet
waistcoat, and a silver-laced hat, and appeared
by his looks to be about thirty years of age.'
Here is another : ' Last Sunday night a gentleman was attacked in Mary's Lane by two fellows with an intent to rob him ; he seized one
of them and threw him into a cellar, but the
other knocked him down. He soon recovered
himself, and boldly attacked them again ; upon
which they made off, but he still pursued, and
took one of them, and called a watchman, who
was only a short distance from him, but would
not come to his assistance ; the gentleman was
obliged to let the villain go, on some ruffians
coming up. He lost his watch and buttons,
but the next morning found them in some mud
where he had been knocked down. The same

day a woman, genteely dressed, was detected
for picking the pocket of a gentlewoman in
Liffey Street, out of which she had taken fifteen
shillings, and upon searching her, half a crown
was found in her shoe and half a pistol in a
snuff-box ; the rest she lost in the hurry.   The
populace dragged her to the quay, tied a ship's-
rope round her, and ducked her severely.'   A
few days later we read that ' some rogues attempted to rob the house of Mr. Preston in
Little Butter Lane, but by the courage of his
daughter were prevented from accomplishing
their design, — who, on hearing a noise, got
out of bed, charged two pistols, opened the
parlour window, and fired amongst them, upon
which they made off ; she then charged again,
went upstairs and looked out of the window, in
order to give them another salute if they thought
it proper to have paid a second visit.'   A paragraph which throws a somewhat curious light on
the punishment of criminals, says, ' The woman
whom the watch discharged the other night, and
who was principal in stealing a great quantity
of plate, is the very notorious pickpocket who
goes into public assemblies in fine cloathes, the
better to perpetrate her wickedness, and who
was some time ago convicted of picking pock-
ets, and sentenced to be whipt at the cart's

tail ; but the hangman did not think fit to exe-
cute the sentence, so she only walked after the
cart in a sort of triumph to College Green,
where she was put into a landau, though two
poor devils were almost whipt to death the
same week, not having stolen money enough to
bribe the hangman or some other officer.'

It was not only money and goods, however,
which were stolen in those days, but human
beings. ' Last week,' says the ' Dublin Journal,' August, 1751, ' a man near Aungier Street
desired two little girls to go along with him on
pretence of seeing his wife, whom they knew,
and to bring their caps with them, which they
did; but their mothers, getting intelligence which
way they had gone, pursued and luckily came
up with them on George's Quay, and brought
them back. ' T is imagined the villain intended
to put them on board a kid-ship, to send them
to the plantations in America.' A month later
a ' fellow was taken up in Back Lane for running away with a child from a woman ; and as
it has not since been heard of, he was committed
on suspicion of kidnapping or murdering of it.'
A little while later we read in the same paper
that ' since the late strict and severe inquiry
after the kidnappers, these miscreants have
ceased to perpetrate their villainy, at least in so

public a manner as heretofore ; but we are told that amongst these robbers there is a prime young villain, who sometimes in the dress of a beau, and at other times like a merchant, tells the wretches he deludes that he went a few years ago from Dublin to America, a poor boy, to try his fortune, and that a lady of that country soon fell in love with him ; that he married her and has now many negro slaves under him, and that all the women who transport themselves, especially from Ireland, immediately get rich husbands. Besides this fine-dressed rogue, there are several in the habit of sailors, who pick up poor tradesmen in the street, pretending to know them, then ply them with spirituous liquors and abundance of lies about the pleasures they are to enjoy in the plantations abroad, by which means they delude those unhappy victims into a miserable and dangerous voyage, where they lie during the whole time promiscuously in the hold of the ship, in filth and nastiness, insulted perpetually by brutish sailors, and generally die miserably in their tedious passage.'

The streets were badly lit, ill paved, ' out of repair, and in several places raised to such a height that carriages or horses cannot with safety pass over the same,' whilst the entrances to underground cellars, extending far into the sidewalk, without rail or other protection, were frequently the cause of severe accidents, and occasioned deaths to those who passed that way, as we learn from the papers. Speaking of these mishaps, ' Faulkner's Journal ' says, ' As lives are sometimes lost, and many legs, arms, skulls, and bones of common people broken by cellars projecting too far into the streets, it is most humbly requested by many who wish well to the publick, and are not carried in coaches or chairs, that some of our nobility, gentry, magistrates, grand and *petit* jurors, would be pleased to break a few of their limbs, or knock out their eyes, or brains, and then perhaps laws might be made, or those already in being put into execution against the encroachments of cellars into the streets.' Here is another strange paragraph from the same journal which speaks volumes for the condition of the town : ' Upon account of the many sturdy and strolling beggars, impostors, and idle vagrants throughout the kingdom, the nobility, gentry, and clergy are determined to have all the faces of the men shaven clean ; to examine their tied up legs and arms, to force the tongues of those who pretend to be dumb in order to make them speak, and to detect those vile impostors who pretend to have been sailors, to have been slaves in Morocco and Turkey,

and to have their tongues cut out, — which good
resolutions, if put into practice in city and country, will be a means of ridding this nation of the
vilest miscreants and vermin that infest this earth,
and are the plague and pest of all human society,
having every vice in them without one virtue, as
they will not work, but live on the blood, vitals,
and labour of the industrious poor, who, when
reduced by sickness or want of work, are
ashamed to beg.' Another paragraph declares,
'The Lord Mayor hath given orders that no
coach, cart, chariot, chaise, chair, etc., shall
stand without horses after sunset, before any
coachmaker's or wheelwright's house whatever ;
which will be of great service to the public, as
villains and idle vagabonds often lie in them, and
frequently surprise people on dark nights ; and
sometimes coaches and chairs run against them,
to the great danger of lives and limbs.'

To all classes of the Dublin citizens the theatre
was the favourite source of amusement. So fond
was the polite world of plays that private theat-
ricals were much in vogue in the houses of the
nobility. Frequently, too, at the Castle the
officers and gentlemen of the vice-regal household gave amateur performances ; whilst once,
at least, a play, ' The Distressed Mother,' was
acted in the great council-chamber of the Parlia-

ment House itself.   The *dramatis personæ* were
of the first rank and fashion.   My Lord Moles-
worth's fair daughter played Hermione ; Miss
Parker, Andromache ;   my   Lord   Mountjoy,
Pyrrhur ; and my Lord   Kingslands's   brother,
Orestes.   All   the   bishops,   judges,   and   privy
councillors attended,   besides the whole fashionable part of the town.

Amongst the ladies of quality most attracted
by the theatre and all concerning it was the
Hon. Mrs. Butler, a bright, busy, vivacious
woman, whose husband, Colonel Butler, my
Lord Lanesborough's brother, ' a plain, rough,
merry officer, doated on her, and admired everybody that liked her.'   Mrs. Butler was a frequent attendant at the playhouse ;   and when
George Anne Bellamy had been in Dublin six
years previous to the Woffington's second visit,
this daughter of an Irish peer had been introduced by Miss O'Hara, Lord Tyrawley's sister,
to Mrs. Butler, who at once took the actress
under her social wing, patronised her on the
stage, and lionised her in her drawing-room.
Garrick was at this period, 1745, immediately
after his parting with Peg Woffington, performing for the second time before a Dublin audience, in company with Sheridan, they having
agreed to play Shakesperian characters with him

alternately. The Bellamy was likewise in the
company. As Quin had, on her first appearance in Covent Garden, objected to the lady's
playing Monimia in the same piece with him, so
Garrick, who had but a poor opinion of her talents, protested against her playing Constance
to his King John. Moreover, he desired that
Miss Orpheur, a ' hard-favoured ' actress, would
take the part.

Now George Anne had set her heart on being
seen as Constance, and had secured some very
fine gowns wherewith to dress the character ;
she therefore resented Garrick's objection, and
almost involved him and Sheridan in a quarrel
on the subject, Sheridan having taken her side.
It was, however, finally settled that the ' hard-
favoured ' actress was to play the part ; whereon
Miss Bellamy, who was a lady of spirit, or, in
other words, a little vixen, determined to have
her revenge. She therefore fled to her patroness, Mrs. Butler, and laid full her bitter complaint before that sympathetic lady, who, having
no objection to give proof of the power she ex-
ercised in the genteel world, at once promised
to espouse her protégée's cause. Therefore,
setting aside her partiality for Garrick, she resolved to punish him for thwarting Miss Bellamy
in her lawful desires. To this end she sent

round polite messages to all her friends, re-
questing them, as a favour to her, not to attend
the theatre on the night when ' King John ' was
played. As she was a social power, and gave
prodigiously fine balls, to which admission was
always eagerly sought, her request was readily
complied with, so that on the night when the
tragedy was played the boxes were tenantless
and the pit empty, to the consternation of David
Garrick and the wonder of the world. This
was the first humiliation in connection with his
profession which the great actor ever received.
But it was not the only triumph which the
young lady of spirit secured this season; for
presently Sheridan played King John, and she
Constance, when the theatre was so crowded
that vast numbers could not be accommodated
with admission. Nor was this all. She was of
opinion that Garrick had not yet received sufficient mortification, and so the young actress
eagerly awaited an opportunity of inflicting
more. Accordingly, when Garrick's benefit
came round, he selected to play in ' Jane
Shore ; ' and knowing from experience the social influence which the Bellamy commanded,
and being ever a wise man where money was
concerned, he requested her to play the part of
the unhappy heroine. This she refused ; as she

was unfitted to perform the character of Constance, she, in her womanly spirit, told him she was likewise unsuited to take that of Jane Shore.

But Garrick, unwilling to let his interest suffer, besought Mrs. Butler to use her influence with her protégée on his behalf; in the meantime he strove to make his peace with the young lady, and ingratiate himself in her favour. For this purpose he resorted to flattery, an artifice which in the world's history has so often served to overcome a woman's heart. He therefore wrote to her that if she would oblige him by playing, he would write her 'a goody-goody epilogue,' which, with the help of her eyes, 'would do more mischief than ever the flesh or the devil had done since the world began.' This missive, which contained many similar compliments, was addressed 'To my Soul's Idol, the Beautiful Ophelia,' and given into the hands of his servant to carry to Miss Bellamy. The man, being busy, called a porter, and without looking at the address, bade him deliver the letter. The porter, believing some joke was intended, carried it to a newspaper office, the result of which was that it appeared in print next day. When the story got abroad, the whole town made merry of Garrick's love-letter. The idol of Mr. Garrick's soul was, however, reconciled to him ; no doubt the reference to her eyes, which were beautiful and blue, had the desired effect of softening her heart.

Garrick, whilst in Dublin this season, constantly visited at Mrs. Butler's home in Stephen's Green. The lady was fond of theatrical lions, but, moreover, she liked Davy for himself. Garrick returned the compliment in kind, but she probably had reason to suspect that the complexion of his love was not of the same platonic type as hers, and having some Hibernian humour, she deigned to play him a trick. When he was about to take his leave previous to his return to London, she told him with faltering words she had a sealed package for him, which contained that which was more valuable than life. ' In it,' said she, ' you will read my sentiments ; but I strictly enjoin you not to open it until you have passed the Hill of Howth.' Garrick, having little doubt that this package contained a declaration of her sentiments for him, which prudence forbade her to make known whilst he remained in the same country with her, received it from her hands with a significant glance, and an air of regret that was touching. Next day, when the vessel

which bore him across the Channel had reached
the specified point, he eagerly broke the seals
and tore the cover from the packet, which contained — not the declarations of a broken heart,
but a copy of Wesley's hymns and Dean Swift's
' Discourses ; ' when so great was his chagrin
and disappointment, that he flung both the Dean
and Wesley right into the sea.

END OF VOL. I.